I0729398

Bittersweet Dreams

What would you do if you discovered your fiancé was a thief? Karen Brown's fiancé was the treasurer of their large megachurch. After embezzling thousands of dollars, he disappeared with his beautiful assistant. Reeling from shock, Karen moves back in with her mom. When she arrives, she meets Keith, the blunt next-door neighbor who knows way too much about her past. Keith Baxter—plumber and future preacher—is enamored with Karen. Can he sweeten Karen's mood with his homemade candy and convince her that not all men are dishonorable?

Bittersweet Dreams

The Candy Beach Series

Copyright © 2020 by Cecelia Dowdy.

All rights reserved under International and Pan-American Copyright Conventions.

By payment of required fees, you have been granted the non-exclusive, non-transferable right to access and read the text of this book. No part of this text may be reproduced, transmitted, downloaded, decompiled, reverse engineered, or stored in or introduced into any information storage and retrieval system, in any form or by any means, whether electronic or mechanical, now known or hereinafter invented without the express written permission of copyright owner.

Please Note:

The reverse engineering, uploading, and/or distributing of this book via the internet or via any other means without the permission of the copyright owner is illegal and punishable by law. Please purchase only authorized electronic editions, and do not participate in or encourage electronic piracy of copyrighted materials. Your support of the author's rights is appreciated.

No part of this book may be reproduced or transmitted in any form or by any electronic or mechanical means, including photocopying, recording or by any information storage and retrieval system, without the written permission of the publisher, except where permitted by law.

For more information, or to book an event, contact :

cecelia@ceceliadowdy.com

https://www. ceceliadowdy.com

Cover design by Elizabeth Mackey Graphics

https://www.elizabethmackeygraphics.com

ISBN - Paperback: 978-1-7338926-6-7

First Edition: July 2020

Bittersweet DREAMS

CECELIA DOWDY

Divine Desserts Publishing LLC

Dowdy writes with the right touch to keep the readers engaged and vested... - **USA Today**

1

Karen eyed herself in the mirror one last time. Simple, classy, elegant. She grinned. She looked fabulous in her cream-colored suit and high-heeled shoes. Ever since her date with her fiancé Lionel last week, the Sunday Founder's Day Service at her church had been on her mind. Over a romantic dinner, he'd hinted that he had some big news to share with her after the Founder's Day Service.

She giggled as she got patted her hair, which, she'd coiffed into a perfect French roll. Elegant curls dangled at the side of her head. Strolling as quickly as she could in her high heels, she locked the door to her apartment and got into her car. As she drove to church, she couldn't help smiling. She giggled as she stopped at a light. "Lord, thank you for this beautiful day. I feel so blessed. Amen." As she pulled away from the light, she gripped the steering wheel. *Lord, I'm so happy that I don't know what to do with myself.*

She'd not heard from Lionel over the last couple of days. He'd been away at a finance conference and he'd said he'd be too busy to talk. He promised to make it up to her once he returned. He was supposed to land at five AM that morning. He was meeting her at church for the late service. After church, he was taking her out to lunch at Genevieve's, an elegant French restaurant. He only took her there for special occasions. The last time they'd dined there, it'd been when he'd proposed to her. She grinned as she pulled into the church parking lot. *Lord, Lionel is going to finally set a date for our wedding today.* He'd been hesitant about setting a date. They'd been engaged for months, and every time she'd broached setting a date, he always changed the subject. Well, she knew he wanted to get married. What man would purchase an engagement ring for a woman unless he were serious about marriage?

Before exiting the car, she scrutinized her left hand. The solitaire diamond ring sparkled under the bright sunlight. She'd sit and stare at her ring for hours sometimes. She polished it every night so that it always looked nice. Oh, the ring was so beautiful. The two-carat king looked glorious against her brown skin. Whenever she looked at it, she thought about the deep love she shared with her future husband.

Well, enough time staring at her ring. She shivered with happiness. After they set their wedding date today, she'd order the save-the-date cards and start choosing the stationary for their wedding invitations. She was thinking of cream-colored invitations etched with gold lettering as she got out of the car and strolled toward the church. She stopped walking when she spotted two of her church acquaintances conversing. "Good morning." The joy spilled from her voice like warm, fragrant water.

Both of the middle-aged women looked up at her and then looked away, as if they were hiding something. Their actions reminded her of how she'd acted whenever she'd gotten caught sneaking cookies from the cookie jar before dinner. Both women then glanced her way again. "H-Hello." Their mumbled greeting seemed forced as they blatantly ignored her and returned to their whispered conversation.

Well, that was strange. Looked like she'd been interrupting an intense private conversation. She shrugged as she pushed the church doors open. Mr. D., the usher standing in the foyer, handed her a program. "Morning, Karen." His dark eyes appeared sad. What was wrong with everybody this morning? Mr. D. was always smiling. Maybe something had happened.

"Mr. D. what's wrong?"

"Pastor has an important announcement this morning."

She gripped her program and touched his arm. "Did someone get hurt...or did somebody die?" Quick as she could, she mentally scrolled through the list of sick and shut-in parishioners. *Lord, please let everybody be okay.*

"No. Nothing like that." He then turned toward the next person who strolled into the foyer. Her bright mood darkened, just a little bit, as she strolled into the sanctuary. She'd taken so long primping that morning that she'd barely made it to church on time. Her and Lionel always sat together near the front. Whomever arrived first, would always save the other person a seat. She sighed. No empty seats in the front. Where was Lionel?

She scanned the small crowd. Where was he? Was it just her imagination, or were some of the parishioners giving her strange looks?

She finally took a seat near the back. Her elation from moments ago wilted like spoiled lettuce. Where was Lionel? She pulled out her phone and texted him.

Where are you? Was your flight delayed? Church is about to start.

Pastor Smith approached the podium. Silence filled the church as he adjusted the microphone. "Before we begin praise and worship, we need to make an announcement." He took a deep breath. "We recently discovered that the church bank account is nearly empty."

She gulped and gripped her hands together. Lionel was the church treasurer. Well, maybe he'd....opened another account or something. Once he showed up to church that morning, she was sure he'd straighten everything out. Lionel was a good, honest man. From what she'd always heard, he was the best treasurer that this megachurch had ever had. Her heart thudded as she glanced at her phone. Her text remained unanswered. Oh, where was he?

"We have to speak to our treasurer Lionel Green. So far, our calls have remained unanswered and he's not been at home."

But he was at a finance conference. Didn't he tell the church that he'd be away for a few days? She had to find him and let the church know that everything would be okay. Lionel wouldn't steal money and lie...would he?

She gulped again as she held her phone in a tight grip. The room seemed too warm. The person sitting beside her leaned toward her and patted her hand, as if to offer comfort. She glanced around the church.

Some people were staring at her.

A few of the women glared at her, as if *she* were responsible for the empty bank account. Heat, thick and heavy, swept through her soul. Sweat beaded her forehead and trickled down her face. *Oh, Lord Jesus, I have to get out of here.* She stood up on her shaky legs and tromped out of the pew and down the aisle. Quick as she could, she rushed to the bathroom. She marched to a stall, slammed it closed and locked it. She dropped onto the toilet seat, using it as a chair. She couldn't pray, couldn't even think. Pain shot through her head like bullets. She squeezed her eyes shut. Her shoulders shook as tears slid down her face. She shoved a wad of toilet paper against her eyes and mouth and silently sobbed.

Two weeks later...

Karen shoved the church doors open while swiping away the hot, wet tears streaming down her face. "Pastor Smith, I can't believe Lionel is still missing." Her voice echoed as she ran into the church.

The elderly reverend and his wife, Candace, hugged Karen, patting her back. After they released her, Candace stroked Karen's shoulder. "Honey, something has just come to our attention."

"What's that?"

"The way we announced Lionel's disappearance and the empty bank account at church two weeks ago. The pastor and I were under the mistaken impression that you'd already been informed. Tara later told us that she couldn't contact you. She'd tried to call you but didn't get an answer."

She sighed, frowning. "But, I didn't receive any phone calls."

"Honey, we just realized that nobody spoke to you directly about this before we announced it. Tara insisted that she called you and left messages. We were shocked when you showed up at church that morning. We were also surprised that you didn't know. It was unkind to deliver the news the way that we did."

Well it was a moot point now. All they needed to do was focus on finding Lionel and figure out what happened. Candace pointed down the hall. "The police detective is in the boardroom, waiting to talk to you. Are you sure you're up for this?"

Karen wiped her eyes again and took a deep breath. *Lord help me.* She squeezed her hands into fists and took another breath. She really needed to get ahold of herself. The traumatic events which had occurred over the past couple of weeks played through her mind like a nonstop movie. She winced and moaned. Her fiancé, Lionel Adams, had been fired as church treasurer after being accused of stealing thousands of dollars from their megachurch. And it was rumored that the assistant treasurer, Michelle

James, had aided him with the theft.

Like the rest of the congregation, Karen had been shocked when the allegations against Lionel were initially announced at church.

Karen turned toward Candace. She covered her trembling lips with her hand. "I'll— I'll do the best I can to—to answer his questions."

The threesome slowly exited the sanctuary and walked down the hallway, toward the boardroom. A moment later, the pastor stopped outside a closed door, placing his hand on Karen's shoulder. "Karen, Michelle is missing also."

Karen gasped, stepping away from the pastor. "That. . .that can't be true." She'd refused to believe the rumor that Michelle had aided Lionel with the alleged theft.

He nodded. "Unfortunately, it is." He took a deep breath. "The church leadership team is concerned for both her and Lionel's welfare. We want to find them, but we can't ignore what's happened."

Candace took her hand. "Honey, we have to do all we can to locate them.

What if there was foul play involved? Don't you want to make sure Lionel is safe?" More tears rushed from Karen's eyes, and she wiped the moisture away. Her head pounded as she leaned against the cool wall. She really needed to calm down. She focused on the coolness of the tiled wall against her hot skin.

Pastor Smith touched her shoulder. "Are you okay?"

Pulling herself away from the wall, she sighed. *God, give me strength.* "I–I'm okay now."

The pastor gestured toward the door. "The detective is in here. We called you to be questioned first since you know Lionel so well."

Karen glanced at Candace. "Nobody told the congregation exactly how much money Lionel may have stolen. We just know it was thousands of dollars. How much cash was missing?"

The woman released Karen's hand and looked at her husband, frowning. The pastor paused before speaking. "Fifty thousand dollars."

The room swayed as Karen leaned against the wall. Her head started spinning, as if a vicious cyclone spun in her brain. She whimpered and turned away. "Lord, please help me deal with this pain."

Candace patted her shoulder. "We'll take this one day at a time. The Lord will see us through."

Karen glanced at the closed door. How in the world would she find the courage to go in there? She rubbed her hands together. A few minutes alone, that's what she needed. After she took some time to settle down, pray a little bit, then she'd have the courage to do what she needed to do. "Is it okay if I go to the restroom before talking to the detective?"

Candace nodded. "Of course."

Leaving the couple, Karen walked to the bathroom, pushed the door open, and entered the room, desperately seeking a private moment with the Lord. Her heart skipped a beat when Tara Baker, the church secretary, dressed in an immaculate cream-colored suit and sporting stylish hair and polished fingernails, stepped out of the stall. Spotting Karen, her dark eyes widened.

While the secretary wordlessly

washed her hands, Karen regarded her own worn jeans and faded T-shirt before touching her hair, which she'd pulled into a ponytail in her haste to get to the church. Maybe she should've taken time to change and freshen up before coming to the church.

"I always thought Lionel and Michelle were up to no good." Tara mumbled, drying her hands with a paper towel while glaring at Karen.

Could this day get any worse? Karen gritted her teeth. How in the world could Tara be so rude? As a Christian, she should've been offering her warmth, support, prayer…not cold rudeness. She opened her mouth, about to give this woman a piece of her mind, but Tara narrowed her eyes and leaned toward her.

"I find it hard to believe that you had no clue what your fiancé was doing behind your back." She was about confirm if Tara had tried to reach her when Lionel went missing. Before Karen could speak, Tara turned on her heels and strode out of the restroom.

Waves of pain floated through Karen's

head as she struggled to blot out the secretary's unkind words. She squeezed her eyes shut and bowed her head. She needed to focus on Jesus right now. "God, please help me. Help us to find Lionel and Michelle. And keep them safe. Amen." Somewhat soothed, she rejoined the pastor and his wife.

Pastor Smith gestured toward the now-open door. "Karen, I'm so sorry about this."

Karen forced herself to smile before entering the room, silently praying for strength. The detective sat in a chair near the front of the room.

The minister gestured toward Karen. "Detective Ramsey, this is Karen Brown."

"Good morning, Karen." The dark-skinned, bald detective nodded toward her.

"Good morning," Karen mumbled, taking a seat near the detective. She turned to her minister. "Can you stay here with me, Pastor Smith?"

The clergyman touched her arm, gazing at the detective. "Is that okay with you, detective?"

Ramsey shrugged, opening his notebook. "If she wants you to stay, that's fine."

Pastor Smith settled into the empty chair beside her.

The investigator asked his first question. "Do you know where Lionel is?" "I. . ." She paused, chewing on her lower lip. "Before the church announced that he was fired, he told me he was going to go out of town for a conference and he said he'd visit his cousin for a few days afterwards. I haven't talked to him since, and th–that was over two weeks ago." She paused, gripping the arms of the chair. "I—I haven't been able to contact him since he left." She took a deep breath. "He won't answer his cell phone. I figured he wanted some time alone and I would see him when he returned for his hearing."

The detective looked up from the notes he was writing. "Where does his cousin live?"

As Ramsey's questions went on and on, Karen felt overwhelmed with worry, fatigue, and nausea. Hot tears flowing down her cheeks, she prayed, *Lord, will*

I ever feel normal again?

Her head pounded with pain, and she began rubbing her temples. Pastor Smith touched her elbow. "Are you all right?"

"My head. . .hurts."

"Detective, is it okay if we stop the questioning for a few minutes while I get Karen some Tylenol?"

"I don't mind at all."

Karen heard Pastor Smith's retreating footsteps as she closed her eyes and rubbed her aching head. Her pain worsened as she leaned back into the chair. Darkness, like a descending hoard of black birds, closed around her. *Lord, God, Almighty, I'm about to pass out.*

2

One month later...

Karen pulled into her mother's driveway, gravel crunching beneath her car's tires. Yellow, pink, and white tulips dominated the front yard, their enticing sweet scent beckoning, welcoming her home. Staring at the blossoms, she tried to relax after the two-and-a-half-hour drive from Ocean City. She loved the beach and she'd miss the beautiful, touristy town of Ocean City. Goodness, she needed some rest and relaxation so while she was in Annapolis to live with her mom, she'd be sure to visit the beach at Sandy Point State Park. She figured she'd go and visit within the next few days, maybe take a dip in the water and soothe her frazzled nerves.

She took a deep breath, stepped out of the car, and walked to the front steps of her childhood home. It had been over a year since she'd been here, and with her present state of mind, the sudden comforting and nostalgic feelings gave her unexpected strength, making her glad she'd decided to return to Annapolis.

Continuing to enjoy the heady scent of the flowers, she unlocked the door and entered the living room. A thud sounded from the kitchen. She rushed into the adjoining room. "Mom?" Her heart skipped when a large, brown-skinned man pulled his head out from beneath the kitchen sink and turned toward her. His light brown eyes twinkled behind his round-framed glasses. He winked at her, quick as could be. Whoa, no way was this man flirting with her right in the middle of her mom's kitchen. Heaven help her, his perfect features, strong jaw...and...good gracious, he smelled delicious, like fresh lemons and...why, this man smelled like lemons and chocolate.

She shook her head. She was simply tired from her long drive and she needed to rest. Her mind was playing tricks on her. This gorgeous man was appraising her, smiling.

"Who are you?" The question tumbled from her mouth like a hard stone.

He dropped his tool and rose from the floor. "I'm Keith Baxter, your mother's next-door neighbor. You must be Karen."

Surprised, she tried not to stare at the tall, attractive stranger. "My mother never mentioned you to me before."

"Well, she's mentioned you to me, dozens of times."

She placed her hands on her hips. "Where is my mother?" Her mom wasn't one who could keep a secret. The thought of her mom, sharing all that had happened with Lionel, with this stranger filled her with unease.

"She's at Bible study over at the church. She asked me to stay and fix her sink while she was out. Said she'd be gone about an hour."

Karen huffed, dropping her purse on the table. *Great, just great. When I need Mom the most, I'm left here alone with a complete stranger.* She sank into a kitchen chair, arms folded, foot tapping. "How much longer are you going to be?"

The plumber narrowed his gorgeous eyes, scanning her from head to toe. "Did you wake up on the wrong side of the bed this morning? You're sure in a sour mood."

She closed her eyes, mentally counting to ten. *Lord, forgive me for my sharp words.* Since Lionel's disappearance her moods had altered drastically. She'd hoped and prayed she'd be over Lionel's deception by now, but so far, animosity toward her fiancé consumed her, affecting her interactions with others. She opened her tear-filled eyes and blinked, again realizing that Lionel was gone. Did that mean they were no longer engaged? How did you break a commitment when your future mate disappeared?

The repairman pressed a tissue into her hand.

Resigned, Karen blew her nose, wondering if she would ever stop crying over Lionel. She turned away, ashamed of her abrupt and rude behavior. After wiping her tears, she glanced at the stranger. "Look, what's your name again?"

He plopped into the empty chair beside her. The delicious scent of lemons and chocolate enticed her. She tried to ignore the intoxicating scent while getting her emotions under control.

"I'm Keith Baxter." His deep voice, soft and comforting, wrapped around her like a warm snuggly blanket.

"Well, Keith, I'm sorry I snapped at you. It wasn't intentional, but I just really wanted to spend some quiet time with my mom." Sniffling, she glanced around the spotless kitchen. "I'm just surprised she's not here."

"Did she know you were coming?"

She shook her head. "Not really. I'd told her I was coming the day after tomorrow, but I decided to make the trip a little earlier." She paused for a few seconds and shrugged. "I didn't bother leaving her a message when I called last night. She doesn't always answer her smart phone." As far as she knew, her mom usually didn't check her phone to see if she'd missed any calls.

"She was at the church until late. The women's choir is rehearsing for the Easter Sunday service in a few weeks."

She fingered her engagement ring. Maybe it was time for her to remove it. Whenever she'd tried, she always lost her nerve. The large beautiful stone was a reminder of all she'd lost. "I didn't realize my mother had joined the choir."

Curiosity sparkled from his caramel-colored eyes. He studied her as if she were a fascinating creature from which he longed to unlock answers to unasked questions. "So, how long are you going to visit?"

She continued toying with her ring. "I'm not here to visit. I'm here to stay."

"You're going to live here? For how long?"

She shrugged. "I don't know. It's hard to say."

"Your mom told me you've been going through a lot with your ex and all."

She gasped. "Why would she tell you about that?" Figures her mom wouldn't keep that information to herself. She sighed. "I wonder if she told anybody else."

He shrugged, still studying her. "I'm not sure why your mom confided to me, but I don't think she told anybody else."

Well, that's a small measure of comfort. Wonder why Mom would tell this guy anything about my life. Just how close is Mom to Keith Baxter, anyway? Before she could voice her thoughts, the front door opened.

"Karen?" Her mother rushed into the kitchen.

"Mom." Karen's voice echoed in the kitchen as she hugged her mother as hard as she could. She sighed. Finally, it was nice to be with her mom, back home. For a long moment, they continued to hold each other. A loud clunk resounded from under the sink as Keith resumed his repair.

Her mother finally released Karen and walked toward Keith, touching him on the shoulder. "Hi, Keith. Thanks for staying to fix my sink."

He poked his head out from underneath the sink, giving her mother a warm smile. "You're welcome. I shouldn't be too much longer."

As he continued his work, her mother led Karen into the living room.

Karen fingered her mother's short, stylish gray tresses. "Mom, you cut your hair."

"Do you like it? I got so tired of wearing my hair back in that bun. I'm much too old to have that much hair anyway."

"It looks nice. It's just such a big surprise." Karen smiled, recalling how her father loved her mother's long hair. "Keith told me you've joined the choir, too."

"Well, it was time for me to get out of my rut."

Her mom patted her arm. "You know Karen, when I saw your car in the driveway, I was surprised. Why didn't you tell me you were coming today?" Before she could answer, her mother looked at her closely as they took a seat on the couch. "You look thinner. Karen, if you don't start eating something, you'll fade away to nothing." She shook her head, her dark eyes sad.

"Mom, so much has been happening." Karen glanced toward the kitchen, lowering her voice. "And I don't feel comfortable talking to you with that guy in the kitchen. He might hear us. Can we go into my old bedroom where there's more privacy?"

"Of course, dear, if you'd like."

Seconds later, they entered her childhood bedroom. The familiar twin bed and cream-colored walls soothed her frazzled nerves. Lying back onto the mattress, Karen rested her head on the fluffy pillow. "I feel so tired."

"You look tired." The older woman peered at Karen. "Now tell me what's on your mind, child. You've barely spoken to me since Lionel disappeared. And the few times I've managed to get you on the phone, you just tell me that you're fine." She sighed. "But I know better."

"I'm handling things, Mom."

"Humph. No, you're not. You didn't even want to tell me what had happened with Lionel. If it hadn't been for your friends Monica and Anna, I wouldn't have known a thing."

Karen frowned, her eyes resting on the emerald green curtains. "They should have minded their own business. I would have told you when I was ready."

"Pumpkin, they were worried about you. I'm glad they told me."

"Listen, Mom, before we start talking about Lionel, I want to know why *you* have some strange man in your house when you're out at Bible study."

Her mother wrinkled her nose. "Strange man? Keith is my friend. And my next-door neighbor." She touched her daughter's hand. "Remember I told you I joined a new church?"

"I remember."

"Well, Keith is a member there."

"Mom, the man had the nerve to mention Lionel." Her voice wavered. "H–he's a stranger to me, and you–you've aired my dirty laundry to him?"

"Karen, I happened to mention it to Keith the day after Monica and Anna called. I didn't tell anybody that you know."

Karen blew air through her lips. This was highly upsetting. Whenever she happened to run into Keith, the first thing he'd probably recall was her terrible situation with Lionel. "Well, how do you know he didn't tell anybody? In this neighborhood everybody seems to know everyone else's business."

Her mom touched her shoulder. "Honey, please don't get so worked up over such a small thing. Keith is very blunt, and he doesn't always think before he speaks. But he's a good Christian man, and his heart is in the right place." She rubbed her daughter's shoulder. "He's been a blessing since he moved in six months ago. He's a plumber, and he's good at fixing other things, too. This house is over fifty years old, and things are falling apart. He's been helping me out a lot." She pulled Karen into a hug. "That's enough talk about Keith. I'm sorry I told him your business. Now why don't you tell me about Lionel? I've been praying for you, hoping you would find the courage to tell me how you've been doing. It hurts that you shut me out of your life after Lionel disappeared."

Taking her mother's hand, Karen's voice softened. "Mom, I'm sorry. I—I haven't really spoken to anybody about what happened, except for Monica and Anna—and the police. They know all about it, but I—I haven't told them how I *really* feel." She lowered her voice. "I've stopped going to church. Mom, it just hurts too much. A lot of the people look at me like they feel sorry for me, and some people act like I'm responsible for Lionel's actions." Her voice wavered, hardening like stones. Astounding to find such unchristian behavior within her own church. "The church secretary wonders why I didn't realize that Lionel was so dishonest. I overheard one woman talking to somebody when I was in the bathroom stall. She wondered if I'd helped Lionel steal from the church and if I knew of his whereabouts." She shivered. "I don't need their false accusations, and I certainly don't want their pity. I can't go back there, Mom."

A brisk knock at the door interrupted Karen's tirade. "Ms. Doris, your sink works. You can give it a try if you like."

"Thanks, Keith. Is it okay if I come to your

house later to pay the bill?"

"No problem." Seconds later, the heavy clomp of boots against hardwood floors echoed in the house.

After hearing the door shut, Karen focused on her mom. "Oh, Mom, couldn't he have waited until we were done talking before he interrupted us?"

Her mom frowned. "Lionel's disappearance has gotten you into a tizzy. You're usually not so sour."

Karen stood and walked to the window. She lifted the curtain and spotted Keith going to his driveway. In front of his house, an ivory van, emblazoned with Baxter's Plumbing in black script lettering, rested next to a sporty black car. After placing a toolbox into the back of his van, he turned toward her window and looked right at her. Even from this short distance, his light brown eyes seemed to pierce deep into her soul. Then, quick as could be, he winked at her.

Her heart skipped. Surprised, she couldn't do anything. She wasn't imagining things. This man had brazenly winked at her twice and he didn't even know her. The nerve....

He grinned and waved before getting into his work van and driving away. Somewhat embarrassed, she dropped the curtain.

3

Well, she didn't have time to think about how this handsome plumber could so brazenly flirt with her. She couldn't let him get under her skin. She had other things to worry about. Pushing the plumber out of her mind, she refocused on her dilemma. "Mom, I'm having the hardest time forgetting about Lionel. I don't think I ever want to go back to his church."

"You don't have to go back if you don't

want to. The Lord won't mind if you choose to worship elsewhere. What about your old church home? The one you used to attend with Anna and Monica."

"I went back a few times, but everybody there had heard about Lionel's shenanigans. I just felt so embarrassed, wondering what they were thinking about him, me. . .everything."

"Honey, you shouldn't feel that way. As Christians, we're supposed to be there to support each other during bad times."

Karen shrugged her mother's comment away. She sat on the bed, bittersweet dreams of all she'd lost with Lionel littering her brain. The scenes from their time together played in her mind constantly, trapped inside her head. She'd dreamed of marrying him, purchasing a large house, having kids together, worshipping together…those wonderful sweet dreams were now soured with bitterness and pain. She swallowed and tried to push those bittersweet dreams out of her mind. She focused on her mom. "I loved Lionel so much. It–it's hard for me to let him go."

"Pumpkin, I'm not surprised. You're in love with him, and you were planning on getting married, raising a family."

"I feel terrible. Sometimes I wonder. . ." She gripped the pillow. "I wonder if he was taken against his will. Maybe he was forced to take that money, and he's being held captive."

"Oh, Karen."

Karen squeezed her hands together. "Mom, I can't help it. What if Lionel didn't take that money and he's innocent?" Even as she said the words, she sensed they were untrue. The evidence was gathered, and it appeared he'd taken the money. She frowned, recalling other things members of the congregation speculated about. Some of the accusations they'd been flinging against Lionel made Karen again wonder if she should remove her engagement ring.

"What's wrong, Karen?"

Karen stroked the floral bedspread, finding the courage to reveal the recent news. "Remember when Lionel disappeared, the assistant treasurer, Michelle James, disappeared also?"

"Yes?"

"Well, the police and Pastor Smith finally found Michelle's mother. Mrs. James has been out of the country for the last month.

She didn't even realize her daughter was missing until she returned to the States."

"How awful. What happened?"

"Michelle's mother told the police her daughter was having an affair with Lionel."

Doris gasped. "Honey, that can't be true. Lionel loved you—"

"I'd like to believe that, but I'm starting to feel like he didn't. Maybe he was going to break our engagement and marry Michelle."

"Did Michelle's mother have any proof of these allegations?"

Karen nodded. "She had personal e-mails that Lionel had sent to her daughter. Michelle had forwarded them to her."

"Have you seen these e-mails?"

"No, but I've heard about what's in them. It's quite obvious they were sharing more than just a business relationship." Karen couldn't help the bitter tone in her voice. *Oh God, why have You allowed this?*

Her mom pulled her into another hug. "Just leave it in the Lord's hands, and He'll help you through this," she advised before releasing her.

Karen grunted. "That's easy for you to say."

"You know, I suffered a lot when your

father passed away a couple of years ago. Remember, I couldn't work for a few weeks, I was so devastated."

"Mom, I'm sorry. It's wrong of me to be so self-centered right now. I've been so irritable and rude since Lionel disappeared, and I shouldn't be acting like I'm the only person on this earth who's suffered pain."

"That's okay. In time, the pain will lessen, and you'll be able to move on with your life." She paused. "Besides, you should thank the Lord that you found this out *before* you got married. Can you imagine if you discovered these facts about him after you wed and had children?"

Karen cringed.

"Well," her mom patted her daughter's hand before rising from the bed. "Why don't we shelve this discussion for now and have dinner?"

"I'm not hungry."

"Well, you've got to eat. Come on, you can watch me fix dinner, like you used to do when you were a little girl."

Moments later, an exhausted Karen sat slumped in a kitchen chair, watching her mother prepare dinner. Soon, childhood memories swept through her as the scent of meat, onions, tomatoes, and garlic filled the room. As steam rose from the mound of spaghetti her mother placed on the table, Karen's mouth watered. Garlic bread and salad completed the meal.

After they'd said grace, Karen broached the subject weighing on her mind. "Mom, do—do you like living alone?"

Her mom poured two glasses of iced tea. "Well, actually. . .no. Since your father passed, this house has seemed so big. . .and empty. Too empty. But now that Keith has moved in next door and joined my church, I've discovered I like having someone else around."

"Does he visit you every day?"

"He'll stop through often enough. Plus, since I don't drive, I get a ride with him to service every Sunday. He's nice, compassionate, and caring."

Karen sampled her food, savoring the tangy taste of the spices. Smiling, she ate for a few minutes, thinking about her mother's words and the handsome plumber who'd handed her a tissue when she'd cried.

Her mom took a sip of iced tea. "He also takes me grocery shopping every week. We usually do our shopping together."

Karen bristled and put her fork down. "Well, he won't have to take you grocery shopping anymore. I'm here to do that now."

"Pumpkin, he likes doing these things for me. And you know, *he's* the one who encouraged me to join the choir."

"What?" She couldn't believe this. "*Keith* got you to join the choir? How many times have I tried to convince you, since Dad died, that you needed to get out more? *And* join the choir. You have such an awesome voice. But you kept telling me you were too shy to get up in front of the entire church. But now this stranger moves in next door, and like that"—she snapped her fingers—"you're joining the choir?" Karen stabbed a meatball with her fork and lifted it to her mouth, wondering if Keith would be coming by all the time, intruding upon her time with her mother.

Doris raised her brows then ate a few bites of spaghetti and garlic bread, giving Karen a few minutes to calm down. "Well, the main thing is I joined the choir. You should be glad. I know I am. I truly love singing."

Karen eyed her plate of food. "You're right, Mom. Sorry for getting so worked up. I'm glad you're getting out there."

"That's quite all right, honey. I understand. You know, after your friends called me about Lionel, I was tempted to take the train down to Ocean City and drag you home for a visit. A mother's impulse, I guess. Even though I was covering you in prayer, I wanted to do more. I wanted to take care of you."

Karen shrugged. "Well, I'm here now. I—I need this time… Time to try to heal from all that's happened."

"I love that you decided to come home, but I did wonder how long you'll be staying. And what about your job at the hair salon in Ocean City? You told me you have a huge clientele."

"I do, but I can always find new clients here. I already contacted the manager at a hair salon in downtown Annapolis, and they said I can start once I'm settled. Besides, the place where I used to work went out of business."

"Really?"

"Yes, the owner sold the property, so I was going to lose clients anyway if I'd stayed." She sipped her tea. "Mom, I've been so depressed lately that I don't even feel like working anymore. That's when I thought of coming home. I thought a change in scenery would help me to heal."

"Have you been praying about it?"

Karen winced, recalling how the situation with Lionel had caused a rift in her relationship with God. "I do pray, occasionally. But for the last month, I haven't even felt like reading my Bible. I just can't seem to concentrate." Her shoulders slumped.

Doris squeezed her daughter's shoulder. "It hurts me knowing you're hurting so much. I could just strangle that man for all he's done." Her voice hardened with anger.

Karen sat silently, biting her lip. "Mom. . .where did I go wrong?"

"What do you mean?"

"How did I ever make the mistake of getting involved with Lionel? He seemed so genuine, honest, and trustworthy." She put her fork down, thinking about her failed relationship.

"I notice you're still wearing your engagement ring."

Karen toyed with the large diamond, recalling Lionel's bright smile when he'd proposed. Whenever they were out at a social event, he'd always wanted her to show off her diamond. She used to think it was because he was proud of being engaged to her; now she wondered if he just wanted to flaunt the oversized stone. "Yes, I'm still wearing his ring. I've gotten so used to having it on my finger that my hand would feel empty without it." Twirling the ring clockwise, she positioned the diamond so that it faced her palm. "I guess I should remove it. It's just hard to do, especially since I haven't heard Lionel's side of the story."

"They still don't know where he is?"

"No." She fingered the rim of her plate. "The judge issued a warrant for his arrest since he failed to show for his court hearing."

"I'm sorry, Karen." She squeezed her daughter's hand. "Pastor Bolton has been asking about you. I told him you'd been going through some difficult times—"

"Mom, I thought you said you didn't tell anybody, except Keith Baxter, about what had happened with Lionel."

She patted her hand. "I didn't. I'm just saying that I was talking to Pastor Bolton and I told him you were having some problems. I asked him to pray for you. I also placed your name on the church's prayer list a few weeks ago, and"— she dropped her fork onto her plate—"here you are on my doorstep." Her voice filled with awe as she studied her daughter. "I know the Lord must have wanted you to come home and spend some time with your mama."

"Oh brother, Mom, I'm not so sure that's true." She shrugged.

"Sure, it is."

"I'm still wondering why God let me fall in love with a good-looking, smooth-talking man like Lionel, not allowing me to see his true colors until it was too late."

Doris stared at her plate for a few seconds. "Honey, you can't necessarily blame God for everything. There was no indication at all that Lionel was dishonest?"

Karen thought about it then shrugged. "If there were any clues about the flaws in Lionel's character, love made me blind to them."

They finished their dinner in silence.

4

Keith tossed and turned in his bed. He finally opened his eyes and grabbed his phone from the bedside table. He peeked at the time. Two a.m. Ugh, his head hurt. Sleepless nights always gave him a headache. He reached for the plastic bottle and poured two Tylenol tablets into his palm.

As he rolled out of bed, disturbing thoughts continued to haunt his mind like a bad dream. He traipsed to the kitchen. A good cool drink of water. That's what he needed. *Lord, please mend the rift between my brother and me.* Pulling the gallon water jug from the refrigerator, he poured some into a glass, popped the tablets into his mouth, and guzzled the cool liquid. After a second glass, he lifted the window curtain to see Ms. Doris's house. The light was on in Karen's bedroom. *Wonder if her problems are keeping her awake, too.*

He put his glass in the sink and found his way into the living room, turning on the light as he went. He lifted the picture of him and his twin brother, Kyle, studying it closely. The photo had been taken right after they'd graduated from high school. He thought about that joyous day and their college years as well—doing some heavy drinking, eating tons of food, and getting together with his brother regularly to discuss problems, women, and class assignments. Their close relationship shifted when Keith had found Christ shortly before they finished grad school. Kyle didn't understand Keith's deep devotion to the Lord and couldn't comprehend why he no longer wanted to go out regularly to get sloshed.

He sighed and plopped into a chair, thinking about Aaron—a friend, lawyer, and member of Keith's church who ran into Kyle occasionally since they were in the same profession. Aaron mentioned having seen Kyle the previous day at a restaurant in downtown Annapolis. His brother was with a bunch of people and obviously drunk. Keith hoped Kyle hadn't driven home that way, and Aaron assured him that he hadn't. "I saw him leave with a woman, and she appeared sober. I followed them outside and saw her get behind the wheel," he'd explained.

A relieved Keith then told Aaron, "I'd appreciate it if you'd let me know whenever you run into Kyle. He and I have been...somewhat estranged since we graduated from college. And since our father died, it's gotten even worse. He doesn't answer my phone calls, texts, or e-mails. So, I finally gave up contacting him." He'd frowned. "We haven't talked in six months."

Keith placed the photo back on the table and reclined in the chair, staring at the ceiling, his thoughts revolving around Kyle. His brother had always had a drinking problem, even when they were teenagers.

Now he tended to drink heavily in the evenings, after he got off from work. Keith wished there was a way to get him to control himself.

He closed his eyes. *God, please help Kyle. May he come to know You and get help for his drinking problem. And, Lord, my own incessant worrying about Kyle isn't helping anything. I have dreams to pursue. I have a calling. Help me to do what you called me to do. Also, help me, Father to learn to leave everything in Your hands.* He relaxed, breathing steadily.

His headache vanished. He sat at his laptop and scrolled through the different schools he'd been researching.

Divinity school.

His calling to become a pastor – he'd not shared this dream with anyone, not even Ms. Doris. It was a dream he'd been researching, aching to pursue, sensing he needed to take his time and tread cautiously. He would tell everyone about his pastoral dream when he felt the time was right. After he was finished scouring the internet, he yawned and trudged back to his bedroom.

He dropped onto his bed. Drifting to sleep, thoughts about Ms. Doris's daughter slammed into his mind. Goodness, she was pretty. Her smooth dark skin and large eyes were refreshing like an ice-cold glass of lemonade on a hot day. Funny how she'd stayed on his mind since he'd met her.

He wasn't prone to winking at females when they first met but...wow, he couldn't resist winking at her. He could tell she didn't like it. She seemed a bit high-strung, and he couldn't blame her, given all that she'd been through. He wanted to take the sadness away from her dark eyes and make her smile. He hoped he hadn't offended her when he'd commented about her problems. He really needed to think before he spoke.

His breathing deepened as fell asleep. *Lord, please help Karen with her pain. Amen.*

Karen forced her eyes open and glanced at her alarm clock: 6:00 a.m. She blinked, the effects of another sleepless night rippling through her exhausted body. After dragging herself out from between the ivory sheets, twisted and wrinkled from her endless tossing and turning, she dressed then ran her fingers through her hair. Minutes later she entered the kitchen and lifted the curtain at the window. Her mother's array of spring flowers adorned the backyard, creating a carpet of color amid the grass.

Smiling, she reminisced about one of her childhood chores: Always an early riser, she'd watered her mother's flower garden each morning before going to school. She dropped the curtain and turned, her eyes drawn to the canister of coffee that beckoned. Sighing, she decided to water her mother's plants before having her morning cup of java.

Grabbing a light jacket, she stepped onto the small porch at the back of the house and met the cool early April breeze. She stopped, closed her eyes, and inhaled the delicate scent of tulips, daffodils, and lilies. *Lord, thank you for this beautiful day.* She sniffed again. Hey, wait a minute. That smell…that smelled like…the tangy fresh scent of lemon and chocolate intermingled with the scent of flowers. She speared a glance at Keith Baxter's house.

Intoxicating.

When she'd first met him in her mom's kitchen, one of the first things she'd noticed about him was his distinctive scent. She'd initially thought it'd been her overactive imagination, but, turned out she'd not been imagining anything at all. Oh, what was she doing? She didn't have time to think about the way her neighbor smelled. She shook her head. Crazy. All that had happened with Lionel was making her think crazy thoughts. She didn't have time to be curious about her mom's neighbor. Besides, she had work to do.

She marched to the side of the house and unwrapped the hose and turned the spigot on. Pulling the lever on the nozzle, she sprayed a fan of water over her mother's beloved flowers. As the plants bobbed in the early morning breeze, Karen realized how much she appreciated taking care of her mother's garden, spending time alone, basking in the scent of flowers.

When the blossoms were well watered, she turned the spigot off and wrapped the hose around the plastic stand. As she turned to go back into the house, a movement caught her attention. Frozen, she stared into Keith Baxter's backyard.

Barefoot, wearing blue jeans with a white T-shirt, he'd stepped onto the porch, seemingly unaware of Karen's presence in the adjoining yard. A book clutched in one hand, and a small plate of...something, he took a seat, closed his eyes, and tilted his head toward the sky.

Mercy, it proved hard not to stare. Was he relaxing or praying? She stepped back. Should she go back into the house? *No matter what he's doing, I shouldn't be gawking at him like a lovesick teenager.* Quickly turning around, she slipped on a wet patch of grass. "Oh!" She fell, her chest hitting the ground. After lying there for several seconds, eyes open, gasping for breath, she spied an ant crawling across the blades of grass in front of her. She jumped up and the delicious scent of chocolate and lemons intensified as she fell backward into a solidly built body. Her heart thudded as masculine arms wrapped around her.

"You okay?" Keith's charmingly deep voice resonated in the small yard.

"Yes." The single word tumbled out of her mouth as she took several steps away from him, as if he were contagious. *Why do you smell so good?* The question popped into her mind.

His gorgeous eyes crinkled with amusement behind his glasses. It almost seemed as if he *knew* what she'd been thinking. Well, she had her pride. She didn't want him to know that she'd been peering at him, wondering what he was doing...wondering why he smelled like citrus fruit and chocolate. Well, she needed to at least be truthful to him. He needed to know why she was outside standing on a wet lawn at six in the morning. "I was watering my mother's flower garden." She gestured toward her mom's plants.

He glanced at the moist buds then turned back to Karen. "Yes, I can see that."

Silence surrounded them, and Karen wondered if she should make an effort to continue the conversation. Keith beat her to it.

"Have you had breakfast yet?"

"Breakfast this early in the morning?"

He nodded then folded his muscular arms in front of him. "I normally get up at a quarter to five to exercise before going to work, so I'm usually hungry around now."

"Oh." Karen didn't know what else to say.

"So, have you had breakfast yet?"

She shook her head, mesmerized by his presence. He beckoned her toward his house. "Come on, I'll fix us something to eat. I know Doris usually doesn't get up until seven." He glanced at his watch. "And I don't have to be at my first job until seven thirty, so we've got a little time."

Slightly dazed, she followed him to his house, shocked when he stopped beside a clump of tulips near his home. Snatching up the pair of clippers resting on the porch, he snipped one of the flowers, pressing the bloom into her hand. "This is for you. I—I want to apologize for yesterday. Some of the things I said...may have been...out of line. And since we're neighbors, well, sort of neighbors, for now anyway, I'd like us to be friends."

The warmth from the contact was comforting, and for some insane reason, she wanted Keith to hold her hand and tell her everything would be okay.

As he continued standing in front of her, Karen realized he was probably awaiting her response. She clutched the flower. "Thanks. It's okay. I shouldn't have gotten so upset."

He tilted his head toward his house, again inviting her to follow. They stepped onto the large walnut-colored porch, and Karen observed the classy wooden lawn furniture and old-fashioned porch swing swaying in the light breeze. A loud bark resonated from the kitchen, and she stepped back, startled.

Keith looked toward her, reaching for the handle of the screen door. "Are you scared of dogs?"

"No." She regarded the large brown-and-white Saint Bernard, its nose pressed up against the screen. "I don't mind dogs if they don't bite." Her voice faltered as she focused on the large pink canine tongue hanging out of the dog's mouth. "D–does he bite?"

He laughed, a smooth loud bellow that carried over the early morning wind. "It's a she, not a he. And no, Suzie wouldn't hurt anybody." He opened the door, and the canine bounded out of the house.

Karen gasped when the dog pounced upon her, knocked her to the ground, and then began licking her face.

"Suzie." Keith yelled, his tone filled with exasperation, as he pulled the dog off her.

Standing, Karen caught her breath while Suzie jumped up and down, barking. Keith focused on Karen, his eyes full of concern. "I'm so sorry. Suzie hardly ever acts up like that when she first meets somebody." He grinned. Oh my, he had the most amazing dimples. Maybe she should ask him about the lemons and chocolate that she always smelled while they shared breakfast. "She must like you. Must mean you're okay, 'cause Suzie's a great judge of character."

The screen door creaked when he opened it. Karen followed the twosome into the house. "Do you mean to tell me you trust a dog to judge the character of people?"

Suzie sat on the floor, her dark eyes scrutinizing her master.

He poured dry dog food into a bright yellow dish and loaded a red bowl with water. Suzie dove into the food. "Not just any dog. I trust Suzie. She knows a good person when she sees one."

Keith washed his hands at the sink then dried them on a paper towel. As Karen watched him remove a carton of eggs from the refrigerator, the wetness of Suzie's unexpected greeting made her cheek tingle. "Do you mind if I use your restroom to clean up?"

"It's right down the hall on your left."

"Thanks." Karen exited the kitchen, stopping in the living room, observing the black leather furniture and TV coated with dust. On the mahogany end table rested two photos in silver frames. Lifting one picture, she observed two identical handsome faces grinning at the camera. The boys appeared to be around five years old, and one of them was missing a front tooth. She inspected the photo but could not determine which twin was Keith.

She returned the picture to the table and lifted the other. The warmth of the duplicate faces made her stare. This photo appeared to be taken at Keith's high school graduation. The twins' blue graduation robes cascaded around them, and each had an arm draped around the shoulder of the other. She again could not tell which boy was Keith. She finally returned the picture to its spot.

Not wanting to be caught snooping, she made a beeline to the bathroom. While washing and drying her face, she wondered about her mother's next-door neighbor. Did he have a girlfriend? If so, she didn't want the woman to stop by and find her significant other fixing breakfast for another woman. She dismissed the surprising thought. Keith's personal affairs were none of her business. Again, she recalled how he'd winked at her the previous day. Well, if he did have a girlfriend, the poor woman needed to be aware that her boyfriend flirted with other women.

5

Seconds later, Karen returned to the kitchen. Spices lined the counter and the smell of bacon filled the room. The chocolate-lemon scent still perfumed the air with sweetness. He grinned when she entered, his milky white teeth a nice contrast to his nut-brown skin. The effect made her heart race.

He turned a few slices of the meat. "There you are. I was starting to wonder what was taking you so long. I was about to come back there to check up on you." He gestured toward the table. "Have a seat. We'll eat in about ten minutes."

Wow, so pleasing to have a someone to cook breakfast for her. Lionel never cooked. He always expected her to make meals according to his specifications. At the time, it never bothered her, because she loved him and wanted to please him. Absentmindedly, she began fingering her engagement ring.

"Are you okay?" Keith's strong voice interrupted her musings.

Karen mentally shook herself. Since Lionel's disappearance, her friends Anna and Monica said they could always tell when she was thinking about her fiancé. "Your eyes get sad, and you look like you're about to cry," Monica had told her.

She tried to smile, forcing thoughts of Lionel out of her mind. "I–I'm fine." She sniffed the alluring scent of bacon and omelets, mingled with brewing coffee. "I guess I'm a little hungry."

"Good, because breakfast is just about ready." He gestured toward the loaf of bread on the counter. "Do you want toast?" He glanced at her, his eyes twinkling with warmth. "You look like you could use some meat on your bones."

Normally Karen would have been offended by the comment, but the way Keith said it amused her. She smiled. "Toast is fine."

He prepared two pieces of toast for each of them then opened the refrigerator and removed butter and jelly. He placed both containers on the table, and seconds later he presented her a meal, served on a paper plate. As he poured coffee into Styrofoam cups, Karen realized she'd seen no dishes in the kitchen. She couldn't resist asking the question that was burning in the back of her mind. "Don't you have any real plates and silverware?"

He gestured toward a closed door at the edge of the kitchen. "My dishes and silverware are down in the basement."

She gazed at the door, still confused. "How come?"

"I hate washing dishes."

She shrugged. "Just use your dishwasher."

"I do sometimes, but it seems like a waste to run the dishwasher for just one person."

He sat beside her, adding a generous amount of cream and sugar to his coffee. He touched her hand, causing smooth liquid warmth to travel up her arm. Sitting in Keith Baxter's home, sharing breakfast, had a charming and intimate quality about it.

He peered directly into her eyes. "Do you mind if I say the blessing?"

The kitchen suddenly seemed too small...too warm. Maybe after she ate some breakfast, the fluttery butterfly-like feeling would evaporate from her stomach. Her throat had gone dry, so she swallowed. "I don't mind at all."

His large fingers wrapped around her hand as he bowed his head and closed his eyes. "Lord, thank You for this beautiful day and for this food. Also, thanks for letting me share my meal with Karen today. Amen." He squeezed her hand, and she returned the gesture.

"Amen," she whispered. Lifting her plastic fork, she sampled the omelet. "Oh man!"

Keith's eyes widened. "What's the matter? Don't you like it?"

"I love it!" She took another bite and chewed slowly, trying to decipher the ingredients. "What's in here?" The sweet taste of cooked onions, mushrooms, gooey swiss cheese, salt, pepper...and something else. She shoved another bite into her mouth. Usually she minded her table manners, but, this omelet…almost made her want to forget decorum and eat heartily.

He shook his head, smiling. "It's a secret."

"A secret? You've never told anybody?"

He bit into a piece of bacon. "Nope. Although I can't take credit for the recipe."

"Really?" Grinning, she sipped her coffee. "I'll bet your mother taught you how to make this." She shoved another bite into her mouth.

His smile faded. "No, not my mother. Ms. Sonya."

"Who's Ms. Sonya?"

"She practically raised my brother and me. If she hadn't had a husband and family of her own, my dad probably would have had her move in with us."

"So, Sonya was like a nanny?" His family must've been pretty well-off financially if they could afford a nanny.

"She was nanny, housekeeper, cook, and whatever else you want to call her."

"I'm sure having Sonya around made things a lot easier for your mother." She wondered what Keith's mother was like.

"My mom died when I was three. I don't

remember her. I think that's when my father hired Ms. Sonya."

"My goodness." Karen couldn't imagine not knowing one's mother. Her parents had always been such a big part of her life that she'd pretty much taken their presence for granted until her father died. "Did your dad talk about your mother a lot? Do you have pictures, stuff like that?"

Nodding, he took another bite of his food then swallowed. "I have lots of pictures, but I don't think my dad liked to talk about Mom very much."

Karen wanted to ask why but didn't want to appear too nosy.

Keith gave her a sideways look. "Your mother reminds me of her."

"I thought you didn't remember your mother."

"What I meant was that Doris reminds me of Ms. Sonya. They don't look at all alike, but your mom's mannerisms, her habits—stuff like that reminds me of Ms. Sonya."

She couldn't stop herself from voicing her next question. "Is that why you're so close to my mom?"

He shrugged. "I guess. I never really thought about it before. The relationship I have with your mother, I mean. It just kind of happened after I moved in. I think our worshipping at the same church, and her needing rides to service, might have had something to do with our spending time together and talking. I know she's proud of you and worries about you a lot."

Karen almost choked on her coffee. "What? She worries about me?"

"Has been, for a long time." He hesitated. "You haven't been down to visit her."

"Well, she took the train and came to visit me a couple of times. So, it's not like I haven't seen her at all for the last year." She decided it was time to bring the subject of her mother to rest. "I saw your pictures in the living room. You have a twin brother?"

"Yes."

When no details were forthcoming, she asked another question. "What's his name?"

"Kyle."

"The two of you look like you're pretty close in the picture." He continued to eat, not commenting.

"Has my mom ever met your brother?"

"No, she hasn't. He's been pretty busy lately and hasn't visited in a long time."

"That happens sometimes. People get tied

up with careers and other things."

Silently they continued to eat. He finished his coffee and poured another cup. "Would you like some dessert?"

"Dessert after breakfast?" She'd never heard of such a thing. Who ate dessert after breakfast?

He opened the refrigerator and removed a glass bowl covered with Saran Wrap. The bowl contained…well, it looked like perfectly round balls of milk chocolate. He tore the Saran Wrap off the bowl and the amazing lemony chocolate smell practically shouted from the bowl. "These are chocolate lemon buttercreams. I got up extra early and made a batch this morning. I make them quite often." His deep voice filled with pride as he stared at the bowl of candy.

"You can eat this whole bowl of candy yourself?"

He shrugged. "It stays fresh in the fridge. Sometimes, I take a batch to church to share at meetings. Like yesterday, I made a batch and shared it at a youth group meeting." Well, that explained why he'd smelled of lemons and chocolate the previous day. She glanced at his shirt and noticed that it was stained with chocolate and yellow. She figured he was messy and spilled chocolate and lemon filling on his shirt when he made the candy. That's why he smelled so amazing. He pushed the bowl closer to her. "Have some."

He didn't have to ask her twice. Curiosity and…something else seemed to erupt within her as she selected one of the balls of candy. She'd never met a man who cooked like Keith Baxter and made his own candy. She bit into the chocolate.

Oh. My. Goodness.

The fresh lemon cream center coated with milky chocolate exploded in her mouth like a cloud of perfect sweetness. She moaned and finished the piece of candy in two bites. Chocolate had melted on her fingers, and heaven help her, she just couldn't resist.

She licked her fingers.

Keith's laughter filled the kitchen. His eyes twinkled and his dimples winked as he looked directly at her. She eyed the bowl. In spite of her full stomach, she wanted to select another piece of candy. But, she couldn't sample another piece. It just wouldn't be right, especially since she'd been so enamored with the candy that she'd lost her mind and had licked her fingers.

Still chuckling, Keith removed a box of aluminum foil from the cupboard. He tore off a piece of foil and, as if he were reading her mind, he placed half a dozen pieces of candy into the foil and wrapped it up. He then presented it to her. Their fingers touched when she accepted his offering. Warm sparks of delight shot up her palm. Her hand felt so warm that she hoped the candy wouldn't melt before she got home. Finally, she remembered her manners. "Thank you."

His eyes twinkled as he quickly winked at her. "You're welcome." When Suzie marched to the table, barking, Keith dropped a piece of bacon on the floor. The dog gobbled it up, begging for more. "That's enough, Suzie." He opened the screen door. "Go on out there and get some air. I'll bring you in before I leave." Suzie ran into the yard, eyed a fluttering butterfly, and began chasing it, barking. The screen door squeaked then banged shut. Keith rejoined Karen at the table.

She wanted to know more about Keith Baxter. Just as she began settling in and sipping her second cup of coffee, he the time on his phone.

"Well, I hate to hurry you out, but I have

to leave in about twenty minutes to fix a client's sink."

Karen fought to keep her disappointment from showing. Since Lionel's disappearance, this was the first time she'd felt like herself. She wasn't sure if it was being with Keith or if it was his amazing breakfast and sweet dessert that made her feel this way. It was also possible that being in a different environment, away from the constant reminders of her botched relationship, that made her feel a little bit better.

He gestured toward her cup. "You can take the coffee back to Ms. Doris's with you." They stood. She held the Styrofoam container and plucked her flower and foil-wrapped candy off the table.

He touched her shoulder. "Before you leave, I wanted to ask you something."

"Yes?"

"Since you're just back in town, I wasn't sure if your mom has had a chance to ask you to come to church. How about if I give you two a ride over there this Sunday? I think you'll like the service."

Karen frowned.

"Maybe I shouldn't have asked you."

She shook her head, not wanting to give

Keith the wrong impression. "No, it's okay. I'm just not sure my going would be a good idea."

Keith frowned. "Why?"

She sighed. "It's a long story. And I know you have to get to work."

He glanced at Suzie frolicking in the yard. "Why don't you at least think about it?"

"Listen, I–I'm just not ready. . .to go to church."

His frown deepened. "Ready? What's that supposed to mean?"

Suzie barked, and Keith checked his watch again. "Look, I've really got to get going. Is it okay if I stop by sometime over the next few days and talk to you?" He gestured toward her mom's garden. "Maybe I can catch you when you're out watering your mother's flowers?"

She shrugged, cradling her coffee cup, not wanting to hold him up any longer. "That's fine." She went out the door and, once in the yard, managed to skirt a galloping Suzie. She turned back and waved to Keith before heading home.

In her mom's kitchen, dirty dishes and a stained coffee cup littered the sink, verifying her mother had already awakened. She quickly placed the candy into the fridge. She grinned, already looking forward to having a piece as a mid-morning snack. Peeking through the kitchen window, Karen spotted Keith yelling for Suzie to return indoors. Minutes later, he drove away in his cream-colored van.

6

The next day, Karen pulled into the small parking lot of the unisex salon in Annapolis, itching to unload the boxes of haircare supplies loaded in the trunk of her car.

She entered her new place of employment, which was bustling with activity. Smooth jazz wafted from the sound system, and a ball game played silently on the TV. A group of people waited in the small reception area while ten barbers served customers sitting in black leather chairs. One child fidgeted in his chair as he watched the barber plug in his electric clippers. When the shears made contact with the boy's scalp, the child let out a shriek. As tears began streaming down his face, Karen felt an overwhelming urge to pull the boy into a hug. Instead, she turned her attention to the young dark-skinned woman with plaited hair sitting behind the receptionist's desk.

Karen approached. "Hi, I'm Karen Brown. The manager, I mean, Carol, told me I could start today. Sorry if I'm a little late. I assumed the salon opened at nine. But I noticed the sign outside says eight."

The woman stood. "No problem." She reached out to shake Karen's hand. "I'm Gail. Carol isn't in today, but she told me to expect you. You got your stuff with you? I'll show you where to set up."

"It's out in the car. I'll go and get it."

"I'll help," Gail said then turned and yelled, "Hey, Darren, watch the desk for me! I'm helping the new woman get set up!"

A barber nodded without looking up, continuing to clip his client's hair. Gail followed Karen to the back of the shop then out to her car, where Karen popped open her trunk. Each woman hefted a box and then trekked back into the shop, setting the cartons down at Karen's empty station.

Gail folded her arms in front of her. "We have ten barbers up front. They bring in most of our business. We keep the beauty shop here in the back."

Karen appreciated the space in the large beauty shop area, which boasted eight black-and-steel-colored hair dryers. A separate section held a washer and an already-spinning clothes dryer. The two stylists glanced her way, mumbling a greeting before returning to their clients' hair.

As they returned to the car to get the rest of her stuff, Gail placed her hand on Karen's arm, halting her. "Before you start, I wanted to warn you about one of the other hairstylists."

"Who?"

"Sheronda. She's the heavy one you saw using a flatiron."

Karen held her box, anxious to get back inside. "What about her?"

Gail leaned toward her. "Well, I know Carol told you that you have to provide all of your own supplies except for shampoo and conditioner."

"Yes, she told me that when I talked to her on the phone."

The young woman continued. "Well, Sheronda will sometimes use some of your supplies."

Karen shrugged, used to beauticians borrowing each other's stuff. "So—that's typical."

The girl waved her hand. "No, you don't understand. Sheronda will borrow perm cream, coloring, whatever, and never give it back. You'll have to keep reminding her and practically force her to return your supplies."

"I'll try to remember that," said Karen, smiling.

Gail continued. "Also, she gossips a lot. So, if you don't want your business making its way up to the barbers, then you shouldn't say anything around her."

"Okay."

Karen clutched her box. That old nudging feeling to own her own shop tugged at her. Lionel never liked it when she voiced that she wanted to own a hair salon someday. Well, Lionel was out of the picture...at least she thought he was out of the picture. So maybe she could focus on starting her own business somewhere in Annapolis, eventually.

The girl continued to talk, helping Karen carry the rest of her stuff into the shop. "Since we get a lot of customers who are tourists, we get a lot of walk-ins. Carol says business is never too slow, so that should be a good thing for you. By the way, do you do haircuts, too?"

"You mean like men's haircuts, right?"

Gail nodded.

"Sure. No problem."

"Great, because sometimes when the barbers are backed up, we'll send their walk-in clients back here to you guys. Sheronda does an awesome job with men's haircuts, but Deidre, the other stylist, doesn't like barbering, so I don't send any of the male customers her way."

Karen arranged her supplies and Gail returned to the desk, giving Karen the first walk-in beauty appointment. She soon got into the flow of the shop, and she was glad that she had two walk-ins in a row since Deidre and Sheronda were taking care of regular customers.

When a few whoops and hollers erupted

from the barbers' area, Karen realized that working in a unisex shop would be a different experience than where she'd worked before, a salon that featured a mostly female clientele.

At midday, some of the barbers ate their lunch, laughing and talking as they watched the game on TV in the front of the shop. A few others continued to service clients.

Sheronda and Deidre had just enough time to grab a bite before their scheduled appointments arrived. They sat with Karen in the large employee break room, eating a Papa John's pizza they'd all chipped in on.

As Karen sipped her soda, Sheronda looked at her engagement ring. "You engaged?"

Karen winced. Why couldn't she find the courage to remove Lionel's ring and fall *out* of love with him?

Deidre came to her rescue. "Stop asking questions, Sheronda. You can see that she doesn't want to talk about it." Deidre plopped two slices of pizza onto her plate.

Karen gave both women a warm smile. There was no need to start her first day on the job on the wrong foot. "It's kind of complicated."

Sheronda folded her arms in front of her chest. "How so?"

"It's a long story."

"Humph. That can only mean one of three things." She held her index finger in the air. "Number one, it's a long-distance relationship." She held up a second finger. "Or number two, you're no longer engaged and just don't want anybody to know." She held up a third finger. "Or number three, the man is in prison and you're too ashamed to admit it."

Karen took a shaky breath. *Sheronda's last assumption isn't far from the truth. If Lionel is ever found, he could end up in prison.*

Gail entered the break room, giving Karen a much-needed reprieve. "Sheronda, your twelve thirty appointment is here."

Sheronda threw her plate away and headed to her station.

Deidre touched Karen's shoulder. "Don't worry about Sheronda. She's just always trying to start trouble."

"Thanks, Deidre. I'm okay."

That evening, after the shop had closed, Karen didn't feel like going home. She drove to the Eastport section of downtown and parked. Wandering the redbrick streets, she stopped at a shop window, admiring the lemon-colored summer dress draped around a mannequin. She toyed with the idea of entering the chic clothing store and trying the item on.

"Do you like it?"

She turned, shocked to see Keith Baxter standing beside her, sporting a pair of jeans and a collared shirt. "What are you doing here?"

He grinned when he looked at her. "I had to get a few things for the church from the Christian bookstore down the street."

"What kinds of things?"

"Stuff for Communion this Sunday, like bottles of grape juice and wafers."

"Is it usually your job to pick up those sorts of things for the church?" She wondered how involved he was within the congregation.

"No. But they're a little short on volunteers this week. So, I offered."

"Oh, I see." She glanced toward the dress again.

"Do you like the dress?" He gestured toward the dress.

"Yes, I like it a lot."

"Why don't you try it on?"

"No, the temptation would be too great."

"Temptation?"

"To buy the dress. I don't think I should spend the money."

"I can understand that." They stood on the redbrick sidewalk, admiring the garment. Keith cleared his throat. "Um, would you like to join me for dinner?"

"Dinner?"

"Yes, dinner." His smile looked warm like sunshine. "You haven't eaten yet, have you?"

She shook her head.

He gestured toward the Spa Creek Bridge. "I was going to walk across the bridge and go to my favorite seafood restaurant for dinner. I love their lobster." He touched her shoulder. "I'll treat."

"A lobster dinner?" A slight breeze blew off the Chesapeake Bay, billowing her light jacket. "That's an awful lot of money to spend on a virtual stranger."

He grinned. "Karen." He steered her toward Spa Creek Bridge, "You're not a stranger to me."

When he said her name, her spine shivered and her mouth went dry. She swallowed, trying to find her voice. "I–I'm not?"

His laughter rumbled. "Of course not. You're Ms. Doris's daughter. She's talked about you so much that I feel like I know you already."

Several minutes later, they entered the crowded restaurant. Scents of shrimp, fish, and lobster filled the air, as well as the din of diners' voices raised in conversation.

The host approached, bearing two menus. "Hey Keith." The men shook hands.

"Hey, Jerome."

Jerome smiled, focusing on Karen. "Two for dinner?"

"Yes, this is Karen. Karen, this is Jerome."

Jerome and Karen nodded and shook hands.

Keith scanned the room. "Do you have a table available with a view of the water?"

"I can help you out with that." They followed him to a table with an exquisite view of the Chesapeake Bay. "I'll tell your waiter to bring your bread right away."

"Thanks, Jerome."

Keith pulled out her chair, waiting until

she sat before he settled into his seat. They studied the menus and Karen glanced outside periodically, watching the ships resting on the tranquil water of the marina. "You seem to know the host pretty well."

"Yes, I come here every week, and when I do, Jerome is usually working." He scanned the room. "I love eating here."

Rays from the bright sun spilled through the window, warming their table with light. Karen glanced at the docked ships. "I remember when I came here for dinner in high school. My date brought me here before we went to the prom." Fond memories unfurled through her mind like the sail of a ship. "It was a nice night."

The server placed glasses of water, rolls, and butter on their table before taking his exit.

He focused on her. "So, you've always lived here in Annapolis?"

"I lived here my whole life until I moved to Ocean City." She sipped from her water glass. "Have you always lived in Annapolis?"

"Pretty much, except for college."

"You've only been living next door to my mother for six months. Where were you living before that?"

"With my father."

"Had you always lived with your dad?"

He shook his head. "No. About a year and a half ago, my dad began suffering from cancer. When he got worse, I moved in with him to help with his care. He died six months ago."

"I'm so sorry." Her voice softened. "I didn't know. . . Did my mother tell you that my father died two years ago?"

"Yes, and how hard it was for her to adjust afterward."

"Yes, it was. . .difficult." Karen swallowed the lump in her throat. "H–have you been okay since your dad died?"

He sighed, gazing outside for a few seconds. "Honestly? No. I still think about him a lot. I just find it so hard to believe he's gone."

Karen touched his hand. "I know what you mean. I felt the same way when my father died."

They sat in silence for a few minutes. "You know, Karen, before I moved in with my dad, I lived in a condo. Then when I started taking care of him, I rented out my place. After Dad passed, I just felt it was time for me to buy a house."

She paused, considering her next words. "My mother tells me that you can be somewhat blunt."

"Yeah, why?"

"Well, I'm about to be blunt with you."

He frowned. "What do you mean?"

"Well, you seem to be pretty well-off to be a plumber. You have a condo that you're currently renting, and you own the home that's next door to my mother."

He nodded. "I make a pretty good living as a plumber. People don't realize how much we charge by the hour." He sipped his water. "I also inherited money from my dad."

"Oh." Not wanting to appear nosy, Karen decided to change the subject. "Since you've always lived in Annapolis, I'm surprised that I've never run into you before, like in school. How old are you?"

"I'm thirty, the same age as you. We've probably never met before because I always went to private schools."

"How did you know how old I am?"

"Your mom told me."

She again wondered how much her mother had revealed about her, but their waiter returned before she could broach the subject.

"Are you ready to order?"

"Do you mind if I order for us?" Keith asked her.

"Go right ahead."

She was pleased when Keith took the lead. He ordered lemonade, corn on the cob, baked potatoes, and steamed lobsters.

After the waiter departed, taking their menus with him, Keith asked, "Mind if I say grace?"

"No, of course not."

Keith took her hand and blessed the food.

After echoing his "Amen," Karen pulled her hand away, trying to ignore the tingle he'd left behind.

Keith began buttering a roll. "So, tell me a little bit more about why you're here staying at your mom's house."

Karen sighed. "Well, for one thing, the hair shop where I used to work closed down."

He shrugged. "So rather than find another job in Ocean City, you decided to come back home to Annapolis?"

"I needed a change." She reached for a roll.

He shrugged again. "But why?"

She bit her lip. Maybe having dinner with Keith was a mistake. "Can we change the subject?"

He held his hands up in the air. "Sure, fine with me." He looked at the marina for a long time. "Doris said that you're a Christian. Tell me a little bit about your church."

"I don't go to church anymore," she said in a small voice.

He frowned. "You mentioned when we had breakfast that you weren't ready to go back to church."

"That's right."

"Why? I know you're hurting because Lionel left, but you can't abandon God because of. . .your situation."

She clutched her roll, wondering if Keith knew all of the sordid details. "You just don't know when to stop, do you?" She threw her bread back onto the plate.

"Take it easy. I was only asking you about your church."

She shook her head. "My church is part of the reason why I left."

Confusion crossed his face. "I—I don't understand."

She tried to calm down. "You can be honest with me. Exactly what did my mother tell you about my fiancé?"

"She said you two were planning on

getting married but he left and nobody knows where he is."

"That's all she said?"

He stopped eating his roll, focusing on the ships bobbing on the water before responding. "She said that you implied he'd gotten cold feet."

"There's so much my mother didn't tell you."

"What happened?" His voice softened.

She told him of Lionel's and Michelle's disappearance and the missing money from the church bank account, wrapping up the story by saying, "So it looks like they stole from the church." Tears rolled down her cheeks.

He gave her a napkin and took her hand, his eyes full of kindness. "Karen, I'm sorry about what happened. But you can't abandon your church because of it."

She sniffled then blew her nose, finding a strange comfort in his touch. "You don't understand. I didn't abandon my church. My *church* abandoned *me*."

"Why do you say that?" He squeezed her hand, encouraging her to continue.

"After Lionel disappeared, I couldn't eat and I couldn't sleep. When I'd come to church, people would stare at me and whisper behind my back. Everybody acted so different. I was so embarrassed." She paused. "S–some of the women think I might have helped or encouraged Lionel to commit this crime. But I didn't. I don't even know where Lionel is."

She wondered if she'd revealed too much. But it seemed she couldn't help it. His warmth and encouragement had caused her to completely spill her soul. Suddenly realizing she was appreciating Keith's hand-holding too much, she abruptly pulled her hand away.

He glanced down at the table where her hand had been then looked into her eyes. "You know, when you said you'd stopped going to church, I thought about a scripture in Matthew. The one where Jesus talks about building a house on a solid foundation? If the foundation isn't solid, the house is blown away when a storm comes."

She nodded.

"Well, I think people's faith needs to be strong, just like the house built on a rock that Jesus was talking about. If your faith is solid, then you'd keep going to church. Don't let the church members' attitudes prevent you from worshipping the Lord."

Her mouth dropped open. "You're telling me that I should go back to that church, with all those hypocritical people, people who are accusing me of being a thief?" Her warm feelings toward him vanished.

"I'm just saying that you shouldn't let other people's attitudes make you stop worshipping God. You need to go back to Ocean City, not run away from your problems. You need to strengthen your faith in God and keep right on worshipping Him in your church."

Glaring at him, she gritted her teeth. "Have you ever been accused of being a thief and a liar by your church?"

Keith's caramel-colored eyes widened, the question apparently catching him off guard. "Well, no, I—"

She abruptly stood. "Well then, don't tell me what to do and how to act when you've never been through what I've been through!"

Their server approached, bearing two plates with freshly steamed lobster. She shook her head, no longer wanting to be in Keith's presence. "I'm sorry. I've lost my appetite."

She left the restaurant, her stomach

roiling in anger. When she got to her car, she realized she'd left Keith sitting at the table alone. She hesitated before she drove away from downtown Annapolis, still trying to calm herself down.

When she arrived home, fatigue swept through her like a tidal wave. She went into the kitchen, knowing she needed to eat something before falling asleep. She made a grilled cheese sandwich and ate half of it, feeling guilty about having abandoned Keith in the restaurant.

She pushed her half-eaten sandwich aside. "Lord, why can't I let this go? Why can't I just get over Lionel and his deceit? I feel so bad about getting mad at Keith when he was only trying to help me." She tossed the remains of her sandwich into the trash before heading for bed.

7

Do you understand the power of faith?" Keith eyed his congregation. The entire crowd frowned. His brother Kyle sat in the front row and snickered. His brother stood up and faced the parishioners. Kyle tried to walk out of his pew, but, he stumbled, drunk. Waving his arms, Kyle opened his mouth. Kyle appeared to be yelling, but, Keith couldn't hear what his brother was saying. The congregation scrutinized his twin brother and then, one by one, each of the parishioners exited the church.

"Where are you going?" He stepped down from the pulpit, but, the parishioners didn't seem to hear him. It was almost as if he were invisible. "Stop!"

Keith jerked awake. He took a deep breath – his throat felt uncomfortable because he'd probably been yelling in his sleep. Water, that's what he needed after another restless night. He eyed the clock. Five a.m. He got out of bed. To take his mind off of his terrible dream he recalled the events of the previous evening.

Plodding to the bathroom, he thought about Karen. After his aborted dinner with her, he'd eaten his meal alone. Later, driving down Main Street, he'd seen his brother strolling down the sidewalk, his arm draped around a woman. Keith had pulled over, his heart pounding as he watched the couple enter an upscale bar. He'd sat in his vehicle for a few minutes, wondering if the Lord had presented this opportunity so that he could approach Kyle. He'd silently prayed then decided the time wasn't right.

Not wanting to dwell on his problematic

relationship with his brother, he turned his thoughts to Karen again. So, she was angry at God. Was there any hope in his smoothing things over with her? All he'd been trying to do was tell her to remain faithful to Jesus amid her troubles. But she'd obviously misunderstood. How in the world was he ever going to become a pastor if he botched things up like this? He took a deep breath.

He'd been a failure. How in the world was he going to fulfill his dream, the dream that he felt that God wanted him to pursue, if he made people mad with his bluntness. He sighed again. He'd been looking through different divinity schools again the previous night, wondering if pastoring was his true calling. Would a church even want to hire him?

He dressed, put his glasses on, and brushed his teeth. He opened the blinds and glanced over at Ms. Doris's house. The kitchen curtains were open, and he saw movement in the room. Seconds later, Karen appeared in Doris's backyard. After he'd watched her water the flowers, he removed a square Styrofoam container from his refrigerator. He then wrapped up another half dozen pieces of his chocolate lemon buttercreams. He took both the candy and the Styrofoam container and hurried over to her house.

Karen abandoned the hose when he approached. Dark circles shadowed her eyes.

He swallowed before speaking. "I'm sorry."

"I'm sorry."

They spoke at the same time, and Keith laughed nervously.

"Want to come in for some coffee?" she asked with a yawn.

"Sounds great."

Karen gestured toward the container and the foil-wrapped candy as they walked toward the house. "What's that?"

"It's your dinner." He paused. "And some more candy for you." Thankfully she grinned as soon as he mentioned the candy. "I didn't have enough room in my stomach to eat both meals, so I got yours to go." They entered her home, and he plopped the box on the kitchen table. "I've had leftover lobster before. It should be pretty tasty."

"Thanks. I'll take it with me to work and eat it for lunch."

She placed the container and the candy in the refrigerator then poured two cups of coffee while he sat at the table. She fixed his coffee, spicing it up with just the right amount of cream and sugar, then joined him at the table.

Impressed that she'd remembered how he took his coffee, he took a sip, pleased with the way the brew danced on his tongue, waking him up. "Look, I know you got mad at me yesterday for what I said."

She raised her eyebrows. "At first I was mad, but after I thought about it, I realized you were just trying to give me suggestions on how to get through this. . .difficult time." Her long eyelashes fluttered when she glanced down at the table, and he wondered what she was thinking. "Whenever I talk about what happened, why I happen to be living here with my mother, I get upset." She paused before continuing. "I'm just sensitive about what happened with Lionel, and sometimes people dole out advice when they've never been in the same situation. I'm the victim here, and some people, especially those in my church, don't seem to think that."

He frowned. "The whole church is giving you a hard time, or just a few members?"

"Just a few people. The pastor and his wife

have been more than loving toward me, encouraging me to come back to church." She shrugged and started looking sad again. "It's just too hard for me to go back there." She looked around the kitchen. "Before I went to sleep last night, Monica called me."

"Who's that?"

"One of my best friends. She told me she'd had her baby."

"Well, that's good news."

"Yeah, I was happy to hear about it. But that wasn't the only reason she called."

"What else did she say?"

"It seems the local paper in Ocean City ran an update on the original story about Lionel's embezzlement."

He placed his cup on the table. "Did you find out anything you didn't already know?"

She nodded. "They've hired an outside firm to audit the church's finances. It appears that Lionel and maybe Michelle have been stealing money from the church for over a year. They've found evidence that both were writing checks drawn on the church bank, then cashing them and using the funds for their own personal use. There's also evidence that they were using the church's credit cards for personal purchases." She touched the large diamond ring gracing her finger. "I'm starting to wonder if Lionel was spending some of that money on me. Did he buy this engagement ring with church money?" She glanced at the window for a few seconds. "Lionel always liked spending money, and I'd assumed the money he was spending was his own. It almost sickens me to wear my engagement ring anymore since it may have been purchased with tainted money."

"You don't know that." He gave the situation some thought. "Is the audit done?"

She shrugged. "I guess so. Who knows? I didn't think to ask Monica what else the article said. I could go online and read it for myself, but I—I just can't do it right now."

"You don't have to if you don't want to."

They sat in silence for a few minutes. Karen's lower lip trembled. "I—I just feel so. . .responsible for—for everything that happened. What if Lionel stole that money. . .to buy me things? Like this engagement ring. What if he thought he needed more money. . .to m–make me happy? To buy us a home?"

"But you weren't—you *aren't*—responsible."

"H–how could I have been engaged to a

man I didn't even know? How could I have been so blind?"

He paused. "Maybe you should start worshipping at our church."

"Our church?"

"Yes. The one your mom and I attend."

His suggestion was met with silence. So, he tried another tactic. "Do you feel better since you're living here?"

"Yes, I do."

"Well, our church is small, and we're always looking for some of our members to volunteer in its ministries. If you start coming to our church and find that you like worshipping there, then you might want to consider helping me out with the youth."

She frowned and then stood, topped off their coffee cups, and returned to the table. "Helping you out with the youth?"

"Yes, at Devo every Friday night."

"What's 'Devo'?"

"It's short for *devotional*. Every week we have a youth gathering—it's mostly praise and worship—and the youth can talk about things that are bothering them. My friend Melanie usually helps, but she's been canceling a lot lately. I'm not sure what's been going on with her, but it would be nice to have another pair of hands. We usually have dinner afterward."

"I don't know anything about teenagers."

"Sure, you do. You were a teenager yourself once, weren't you?"

She smiled. "Yes."

"So? Just remember what it was like back then. Sometimes young people get confused, and it's easier for them to talk to an adult other than their parents."

"I don't know," she mumbled. "I'm pretty confused myself right now."

He patted her shoulder. "Just give it some thought. I think it would be good for you."

"Why do you say that?"

"My first minister in college used to say that when you're hurting, you should try not to focus on your own pain. One way to do that is to help others. I can tell you're hurting, and I just want to make you feel better." He paused. "It was wrong of me to advise you to go back to your church where you felt uncomfortable. I've never been in your situation, so I probably should have told you that it would be best if you worshipped at another church where you felt more welcome." He looked down at his coffee. "Or I could have just kept my big mouth shut."

"Why do you care about me—my situation?"

He toyed with the salt and pepper shakers on the table then shrugged. "It's the way I am. I feel called to help people."

She frowned. "Do you mean like a pastor?"

"Yes." Looking into her dark eyes, he decided to tell her about his dream. "I don't know how much your mom has told you about me."

Karen took a sip of coffee. "Well, she told me about how much you love the Lord and how devoted you are to the church."

"Well, I'd like to lead a church one day, if God allows. You'd think at thirty years old I'd have this all figured out, but I'm taking it one day at a time."

Raising her eyebrows, she set her mug back onto the table. "You want to be a pastor?"

"Yes, I do. But I still have a lot of things I need to do first."

"Such as?" He paused, still struggling with what to tell her about his future plans. "You don't have to tell me if you don't want to."

"Well, for starters, I need to learn how to advise people in such a way that they don't end up leaving restaurants in a huff."

She winced. "I probably overreacted."

"No, I can be quite blunt. I need to work on that. Another thing I'd like to do is go to divinity school to get my degree."

She leaned toward him. "Really?"

"Yes, I'm looking into some schools now."

She sat back. "Have you ever preached?"

"Yes, a few times."

She smiled. "How did it go?"

"Honestly? It wasn't bad, but I felt it could be better." They were silent for a few seconds before Keith reminded her about his earlier question. "Just give my request some thought."

"Your request?"

"To help out at the church. I think it'll be good for you."

"I don't know."

"Our congregation doesn't know what happened to you, so they can't hold it against you. Plus, once you start ministering and fellowshipping with other Christians, it'll take your mind off. . .other things."

"I'll think about it," was all she managed to say.

"Okay, let me know what you decide." He squeezed her hand before he left her home.

8

Over the following week Karen worked steadily at her new job. Turning a deaf ear to Sheronda's prying questions and constant gossip, Karen focused on building up her clientele. Sheronda's nosiness caused her dreams of owning her own shop to filter through her mind like slow-brewed coffee.

She'd been researching how to start your own business on the internet. She'd spent a lazy day at the beach at Sandy Point State Park. It was too early in the season to take a dip in the water, so, she'd made herself comfortable in one of the picnic areas. She'd packed a small lunch in her cooler and had brought her beach reclining chair. She'd been rationing the candy that Keith had given to her, eating one piece her day. She'd placed the candy in the cooler so that the ice would keep it from melting.

While she took a leisurely stroll along the cool sandy shore, she enjoyed the last piece of Keith's candy. She loved the lemony chocolate goodness in her mouth as she eyed the beautiful beach. She enjoyed the candy so much that she'd toyed with the idea of asking him to make another batch, just for her.

She mentally shook her head as she made her way back to the picnic area. No way could she ask Keith to make her some more candy. That candy was so addictive. Maybe she could ask him for the recipe and she could make it herself. She mentally shook her head. No, she'd never made candy in her life and couldn't imagine his sharing his recipe. She figured it was a secret, just like his tasty omelet.

After she made herself comfortable in her reclining beach chair, the wind blew. She zipped up her light jacket and pulled out her laptop. She spent her day at the beach reading several articles about owning a beauty salon. When she returned home that night, and days afterward, she read articles and viewed videos online. The articles and videos were interviews with successful beauty salon owners. What she needed was capital. She didn't have enough money saved up for start-up costs.

Her mom had asked her about what she'd been doing online. She'd not felt ready to tell her mom about her dream. Her dream of owning her own shop was tucked away in the back of her mind to slowly grow. She'd tell her mom about her dream when she was ready to do so. At home, she spent lots of time with her mother, much of it in the kitchen, where they prepared meals and conversed about life.

One evening they dined at a restaurant in downtown Annapolis and then purchased dessert at a nearby ice cream parlor. The ice cream parlor proudly boasted about baking cobblers and pies on its premises and smashing them into their homemade ice cream. While digging into a dish of the store's unique and luscious-tasting blackberry cobbler ice cream, Karen sighed. "Mmm. This is so good." She'd requested hot fudge sauce drizzled over her ice cream. The warm sauce paired nicely with the berries and ice cream.

"Yes, it is," her mother agreed. "So, Karen, are you going to services this weekend? You know it's Easter. What a great time to begin worshipping again."

Karen ate a few more spoonfuls of her treat before responding to her mother's question. "Yes, Mom, I think I will."

Doris squeezed her daughter's hand. "I'm glad to hear that." She suddenly frowned.

"Mom, what's wrong?"

"I just wondered about Lionel. You haven't mentioned him since Monica called about the church's audit."

Karen abandoned her spoon. "I'm still angry, but I don't hurt as much as I used to."

Doris hugged her daughter. "Give your anger over to God," she whispered.

Karen awoke at dawn to a sunny and

unseasonably warm Easter Sunday. She stretched and smiled, having slept well.

Hearing a knock on her bedroom door, she grinned. "Mom? Come on in."

Her mother poked her head in. "Sounds like you slept well?"

"Yes, I did. You're up early."

"Yes. For an hour or so already. I just wanted to let you know that Keith is picking me up soon to take me to church."

"You're leaving already?" Karen yawned.

Her mother nodded. "We need to be there early to prepare for the holiday services."

"Are you excited about singing in the choir today?"

"Well, I don't know about excited," her mother said with a nervous smile. "There's bound to be a big crowd."

"Believe me, Mom. You'll do just great."

"I hope so. Well, I've got to get going. I'll see you later?"

"Wouldn't miss it for the world." Karen grinned.

An hour later, Karen pulled into the parking lot of the small house of worship in nearby Gambrills, Maryland. Bible in hand, she approached the steps to the recently renovated building. Tulips nodded in the spring breeze, creating a rainbow of color beside the whitewashed structure. The steeple gleamed in the early morning sun as if Jesus were smiling down on the church.

Taking a deep breath, she entered the vestibule, admiring the cranberry carpet and paneled walls. Karen's heart stopped when she spotted Keith standing at the sanctuary door, holding a stack of programs. The dark suit, crisp white shirt, and midnight blue tie accented his broad chest and shoulders. His eyes sparkled when he saw her.

"Karen." He wrapped his arms around her.

Somewhat stunned, Karen returned his embrace then stepped out of his arms. "Hi, Keith." It sure was refreshing to see that Keith was glad to see her.

"I didn't know you were coming."

"My mom didn't tell you?"

"No." He grinned. "She spent the entire ride going over her choir music." He pressed a program into her hand. "You look beautiful."

She touched her hair. "Thanks, you look nice, too."

He glanced toward the other usher. "Aaron, this is Karen Brown. She's Ms.

Doris's daughter. Karen, this is Aaron."

She smiled, shaking Aaron's hand. Keith clapped Aaron on the shoulder. "Can you handle things alone for a minute, Aaron?"

The tall, dark-skinned man grinned. "I've got things covered. Take your time."

Keith pulled Karen aside. "You're wearing the dress."

Puzzled, she tried to make sense of his words. "The dress?" The delicious musky scent of his cologne surrounded her, and when she peered into his eyes, she realized his face looked different.

"Yes, the dress you were looking at the night we had dinner together?" He paused. "I mean the night we *almost* had dinner together."

Karen recalled their aborted meal with some embarrassment. "Yes, well. . . I guess I couldn't resist. I'm surprised you remembered." Looked like it was a good call on her part, buying this dress. Keith really seemed to like it and his praise made her feel good.

"There's not much about you that I forget." He gave her a smile that made her feel all warm and gooey inside, like the hot chocolate sauce she'd eaten on her ice cream the other day.

She peered at this face. There was something else about him that was different today. *Hmm. He is so nice, and handsome, and. . .* Karen cleared her throat. As she stuffed her program into her Bible, she tried to focus on his altered appearance instead of the effect he seemed to be having on her. "There's something different about you today. What is it?"

"Huh?"

She frowned in concentration while he continued to grin. And then it hit her. "You're not wearing your glasses." Her voice carried and a few people looked in their direction.

"Nope. I'm wearing my contact lenses."

His light brown eyes were warm and rich. The color of his eyes reminded her of coffee mixed with cream. She looked away, needing to get into the sanctuary to find her seat. She glanced at Aaron, who was looking a bit overwhelmed at the huge crowd of parishioners coming through the doors.

As if reading her thoughts, Keith gestured toward Aaron. "Look, I've got to help Aaron. But I'll talk to you at your house later."

"At my house?"

He led her back to the sanctuary door. "Yes, didn't your mom tell you?"

"Tell me what?"

"She invited me over for lunch after service."

With a parting smile, he resumed his station at the door while Karen entered the sanctuary, both floored and excited about their unexpected lunch guest.

Trying hard not to stare at Karen's retreating form, Keith forced himself to focus on the churchgoers entering the sanctuary. Why did he have to admit that he remembered everything about her? He doubted she wanted to hear that.

Finally, as the prelude began and the ushers were about to close the double doors, Aaron drew closer to Keith, saying softly, "Karen's a cute little thing. Are you two involved?"

Rolling his eyes, Keith entered the room behind his friend. "No," he whispered, not wanting Aaron to get the wrong idea. "You know how I feel about dating right now."

Aaron and Keith sat in the back, ready to

assist latecomers who would be looking for seats. The choir voices lifted in song and Keith closed his eyes, taking delight in the joyful melody resounding throughout the church, wrapping the audience with God's Holy Spirit. He finally opened his eyes and focused on Ms. Doris. Her robe drifted as she swayed with the rest of the choral members. Her dark eyes appeared nervous, but when her gaze met his, she smiled, giving him a quick wink, continuing to sing.

The tune carried on and he clapped his hands, swaying to the rhythm. Parishioners stood in their seats, heartily singing along, clapping, and praising the Lord. Keith smiled, joy filling his soul on this Easter morning.

Sunlight streamed through the stained-glass windows, warming the church with light. When the chorus finally ended, Pastor Bolton stepped up to the podium, his deep booming voice filling the sanctuary. "Happy Easter, everybody!"

Several members responded, "Praise the Lord! Happy Easter!"

"It's a pleasure to have all of you here today." He stared at the audience before speaking. "I'd like to invite Keith Baxter to step forward and lead the opening prayer."

Wiping his sweaty palms on his pants, Keith went to the pulpit, trying to calm his frazzled nerves. He walked onto the platform. "Good morning, everybody."

"Good morning, Keith! Praise the Lord!"

"We are here to praise Jesus today." He bowed his head. "Lord, thank You for this beautiful Easter morning, for this day of life, and for the sacrifice You made by sending Your Son. Please be with us as we continue through the day, worshipping You and praising You. And if there are any souls suffering here today, may Your Holy Spirit comfort them." He gripped the podium, his eyes still closed. "In Jesus' name, amen."

"Amen," several parishioners responded.

Pastor Bolton stepped to the pulpit and shook Keith's hand. "Wonderful job, Keith."

"Thanks for letting me lead the prayer, Pastor," Keith said softly to the minister; then he rejoined Aaron in the back of the church.

As Pastor Bolton read the account of Jesus' resurrection in the Gospels, many members expressed their joy over the event that granted eternal life to those who accepted Jesus as their Savior.

"Amen!" cried members from the pews.

When the sermon was over, the pastor gripped the pulpit. "If there is anybody present who has not accepted Jesus, or if you're a believer with something on your heart that you want to let go and bring to Jesus, please come forward."

Keith and Aaron, part of the four-member prayer and encouragement team, stood and walked forward. This was one of Keith's favorite moments during a service. His heart lifted with gladness when a person came forward, wanting to accept Jesus as his Savior.

Several "Praise Gods" and "Halleujahs" sounded from the audience. They continued to chant the song "Oh, What a Mighty God We Serve" along with the choir as people came forward. Keith's heart stopped when Karen walked down the aisle, tears streaming from her pretty brown eyes. She looked like a wounded dove, and all he wanted to do was lift her up and help take away her pain.

A total of eighteen people stepped forward. Pastor Bolton's wife divided the lot into four groups, one group for each member of the prayer and encouragement team. When

Keith led his group away to the prayer room, he said a silent prayer for Karen, who'd been assigned to Aaron's group. *Lord, may her time in prayer with You heal her spirit.*

9

Before going to Ms. Doris's house, Keith changed into his best jeans and collared shirt, still thinking about the events that occurred after the service. He'd prayed with his assigned group before searching for Karen. Aaron found him and gave him the message that Ms. Doris had ridden home with her daughter and was looking forward to seeing him later for lunch.

Still wondering if Karen was okay, Keith

pulled the plastic container of chocolate lemon buttercreams from the fridge. He'd told Ms. Doris that he'd bring the dessert to the meal. She'd mentioned how Karen had been hoarding his candy, eating one piece per day. He grinned while he strolled toward her house. Just the thought of sweet, pretty Karen enjoying his candy…just knowing that his treat brought her a bit of joy each day…well…it just made him glad.

A light breeze blew, rustling the new green leaves budding on the trees. He rapped on Ms. Doris's back door. Karen opened it, her petite frame sporting a pair of jeans and a pink T-shirt. Resisting the urge to kiss her cheek, he stepped into the kitchen. The scents of cheese, ham, and tomatoes filled the space, making his mouth water. "Smells good in here."

"Thanks. The food is almost ready." She tapped his arm, and his skin sizzled from the brief touch. "Is that what I think?"

"If you're thinking it's my chocolate lemon buttercreams then, yeah."

She grinned, her dark eyes sparkling like jewels. "Oh, Keith, your candy is *so* addictive."

He chuckled. "I'm glad you like it. There's

two dozen pieces of candy in there for you."

Her dark eyes widened. "For me?"

"Well, yes. I brought them to share for dessert. I'm going to leave the leftovers here for you to enjoy."

She accepted the container and placed it into the fridge. "Thanks, Keith." She hugged him quickly. Her perfume smelled like flowers. He returned her brief hug. The urge to kiss her consumed him. She ended their hug, gesturing toward the adjoining room. "Come into the dining room."

Happiness and warmth erupted within him like a small fire. Just being near Karen was making him feel a bit off kilter. He focused on the small platter of cheese and crackers in the center of the dining room table, along with smaller empty plates. "Where's your mom?"

"She's on the phone. She'll be out shortly." She gestured toward the platter. "Help yourself. Would you like something to drink?"

"A Coke, if you have it."

She exited the dining room and returned with his soda. He thanked her before he sat, wanting to relish their time alone before her mother returned. "I was glad you stepped forward at church today. Did the prayer session afterward help?" When she didn't respond, he rushed on, wanting to put her at ease. "You don't have to answer if you don't want to. I know it's none of my business."

"That's okay. It's sweet of you to ask." Sighing, she sat in the empty chair beside him.

He admired her red-painted nails when she placed cheese and crackers onto a plate for herself. His heart skipped upon realizing that Lionel's engagement ring was now absent from her finger.

"You know, my mom told me to give my anger over to God."

"And that's why you came forward?"

She nodded.

"Do you still feel angry?"

"Yes. But Aaron told me it would probably take some time for my anger to go away completely. I do feel better about returning to church, and I'm going to start reading my Bible again."

"You haven't read your Bible since Lionel disappeared?" He found this hard to believe.

"Keith, I've all but forsaken God after what happened. I feel bad about it, and I know my anger and resentment toward God, Lionel, and Michelle was making me bitter."

He touched her shoulder, fighting the urge to pull her into his arms. "Don't feel bad about it, Karen. The Lord's already forgiven you." He dropped some cheese and crackers onto his own plate, suddenly feeling awkward. "I know it's hard to lean on God during difficult times. There are things that have happened to me over the last six months that have tested my own faith."

"Like what?" She looked at him, her dark eyes full of curiosity.

"Mostly issues with my family."

"Are you talking about the death of your father and the situation with your brother?"

He frowned. "How do you know about the situation with Kyle?"

She shrugged, immediately putting him at ease. "I don't. I just sensed things were not well between you two. When I commented on the photo of you and Kyle, you didn't say anything. I almost felt like you were hiding something."

"I wasn't hiding anything. I just don't like talking about it. I've been praying about it though."

"But it does bother you."

"How did you know?"

"Because I know you. You're so intent about getting me to renew my faith in God and not let my anger toward Lionel control my life. You've also told me you're concerned about other people in your congregation. If you're so concerned about me, my mother, and the rest of your congregation, then I sense that you care a great deal about your brother simply because he is your brother."

He was silent as he thought about her words.

She touched his arm. "Do you ever talk to him?"

He didn't like the way this conversation was playing out. "No."

"Why not? Maybe the Lord wants you to call your brother and try to rectify the situation."

"I don't think that's a good idea."

"Why not?" Okay, it looked like she was going to keep asking why until he gave her a good reason.

He didn't feel like mentioning that his brother never wanted to speak to him again. Karen wouldn't understand, and he didn't feel like ruining their Easter lunch by rehashing the family drama that had spanned the last several months.

"I don't think Kyle wants to hear from me right now. I know my brother, and when he's ready to talk, he'll let me know."

"I hope things work out with you two. I'll be praying for you."

Doris came into the dining room. "Keith, I'm glad you could join us."

"Thanks for inviting me, Ms. Doris." He stood. "Do you two need help carrying the food from the kitchen?"

Doris shook her head. "Karen and I can handle it."

The mahogany table was soon filled with the delicious-looking food. "Keith, before we eat, would you say grace?" asked Doris.

As they bowed their heads and joined hands, he asked the Lord to bless their food.

A couple of weeks later, on a Friday night, Keith rapped on the back door of Karen's house. This would be her first night helping him with Devo.

When Karen opened the door, she smiled warmly.

He touched her arm, entering the house.

"Hi."

"Hi, Keith." She brushed his hand with her fingertips. "I'll be right back." He watched her go, his hand still burning from her touch. There was something about this girl that sent his heart and mind whirling. *Karen, do you have any clue what you do to me?*

Minutes later she returned, holding her purse and Bible. "I'm ready." Her velvety smooth voice broke into his thoughts.

"Okay then." He grinned. "Let's go." They headed out the back door and into his car. After pulling the car onto the street, he glanced at her. "You know, I'm glad you agreed to help me with this."

"My pleasure."

"How's the job going?"

She rolled her eyes. "One of my coworkers gets on my nerves, but otherwise, it's fine."

"Maybe you might want to look for a job at another salon if this one doesn't seem right."

She groaned.

"What's wrong?"

"Nothing. I know I should feel blessed to have a job, but I'm tired of working in salons."

He stopped at a light. "You don't want to

be a hairdresser?"

"I love doing hair, but I'm tired of dealing with crazy coworkers."

He pulled away from the light. "Well, if you had your choice, what would you do?"

She stared out the window, hesitating. Then she turned to him. "I–I'd like to own my own salon."

He couldn't help smiling.

She slapped his shoulder. "What are you smiling about? You don't think I can do it?"

"I *know* you can. Tell me all about it."

"What?"

"Tell me how you envision your salon."

"Well. . .it would be large and roomy. Glossy pine floors, great lighting, with plenty of mirrors. We'd have somebody specializing in natural hair. Then the others would focus on doing perms and touch-ups, maybe a weave or two. We'd have high-quality hair dryers and blow dryers. There'd be a washer and dryer in the back to wash the tons of towels we'd use." She settled back into the seat, and when he pulled into the church parking lot, it appeared that Karen barely noticed their surroundings as she continued. "My stylists and beauticians would be so good that we'd be booked solid weeks in advance, and word in town would be that my place would be the best place to go to get your next touch-up or perm."

Pride filled her voice and her full, pretty lips curved into a delicate smile. Keith longed to kiss her. His eyes on her lips, he asked, softly, "What would you name your shop?"

Her grin widened, her dark eyes shining with warmth. "I'd call it Karen's Classy Salon." She grabbed his forearm.

"Karen's Classy Salon." He returned her smile, loving her enthusiasm. "I like that."

She still held his arm in a tight grip, and he didn't want her to let go.

Her smile faded as she glanced down at her hand clamping his arm in excitement. She released him, looking away. "I'm sorry. I get so excited when I talk about my dreams that I don't always pay attention to what I'm doing." She turned back to him with an uncertain smile.

He stared at her lovely face, wondering about the cause of her mood swing. "There's nothing to apologize for, Karen. I like seeing you so enthusiastic."

"You do?"

"Yes, I do," he said quietly.

"Lionel never liked it when I got excited." She frowned. "He hated when I spoke about my dream of owning my own salon."

Sounds like Lionel is the biggest fool who ever walked the face of the earth.

"Mr. Keith, are you coming inside or are you going to sit in that car all evening?" Amanda, one of the teens, shouted at him from the steps of the church. Keith inwardly groaned, saddened that the romantic mood had been shattered.

Keith opened his door while Karen exited the car.

"Hi, Amanda." He squeezed the young girl's shoulder.

Amanda nodded toward him. "Hi, Mr. Keith." Amanda greeted.

He gestured toward Karen. "This is Karen Brown. You know Ms. Doris? This is her daughter. She's going to be one of the youth group volunteers."

"Hi, Amanda." Karen smiled, trying to put the girl at ease.

Amanda muttered a hello and fidgeted, so Keith took her a few feet away from Karen. "Amanda, what's the matter?"

Tears came to the girl's eyes, and she grabbed Keith's elbow. "My foster parents are getting a divorce. I'm so tired of them arguing all the time. I don't know what to do about it."

"I'm sorry." He didn't point out that he wasn't surprised.

"I feel so worthless at home. I've been listening to them argue for the last few years. They get on my nerves." She pulled a tissue from her pocket and blew her nose. "My eighteenth birthday is coming up, and you know what that means."

"I know, Amanda. I've already spoken to the pastor, and we're checking around to see what we can come up with within the church."

"I'm so scared. Everybody else looks forward to their eighteenth birthday, but I dread it. The only person who makes me feel good about myself is Ron. He loves me, and he just wants me to be happy."

Gently he advised her. "Amanda, be careful about Ron. Don't hang all of your hopes of happiness on him. Remember to focus on Jesus. All of us here at church who care about you—"

She shook her head, cutting him off. "It's not the same. I'm special to Ron. He focuses on *me*. He makes me feel good about myself."

Oh, no. Obviously he wasn't trying hard enough to reason with Amanda. Keith sensed impending doom. He'd met Ron and was not pleased with Amanda's choice of a boyfriend. "Amanda, why don't you come out to the church one day after school so that we can talk? I can arrange for Melanie, Karen, or the pastor's wife to be there." He couldn't meet with her alone since their church forbade one-on-one counseling with opposite sexes.

She pushed one of her plaits behind her ear. "I'll think about it."

"Do more than just think about it—I want you to pray about it. How about I ask the youth to say a prayer for you tonight?"

The girl looked mortified. "No, don't let them know about my problems."

"Okay. But I'll be praying for you."

"Okay," she mumbled before she entered the church.

Karen approached. "What's wrong?"

They headed for the stairs. "That's Amanda. She's upset because her foster parents are getting a divorce and her eighteenth birthday is coming up."

"What happens when she turns eighteen?"

"When you're a foster kid, who knows?"

Karen held her hand over her quivering mouth. "Oh, my goodness. Her foster parents won't be getting paid from the state anymore."

Keith nodded. "That's right. I've been trying to find out what I can do for her through the church, but so far, I've come up empty. You know, I would let her live with me, but that wouldn't be appropriate."

"I'm assuming she's graduating from high school this year?"

"That's right. But she's not sure what'll happen after that."

"Is she looking for a job?"

Keith sighed, the problem weighing heavily on his mind. "I think the whole situation is so overwhelming that it's hard for her to focus on what to do."

"Has she been a foster child her whole life?"

"Yes, she's been through a lot of homes."

"The poor girl."

"Don't let her hear you say that."

Karen frowned. "Say what?"

"What you just said about her being poor. She hates pity. And being a foster kid already makes her feel like a misfit." He shook his head, the thought of Amanda's boyfriend making him angry.

Karen touched his arm, her cool fingers calming his frazzled nerves. "Keith, what's wrong?"

Her voice sounded soothing, and for a brief moment, he daydreamed about Karen being by his side when they mentored the youth of the congregation. "I'll tell you later," he mumbled, entering the church. The youth stood in the foyer, several greeting him by name. He shook hands with several of the teens, beckoning them into the sanctuary so they could begin their devotional time.

10

Once they entered the church, the band warmed up, holy notes filling the sanctuary. Karen glanced at Keith. "I'm surprised you have a band here tonight."

"A few of the teens play instruments, so they accompany us during praise and worship." As Karen and Keith headed to the front of the sanctuary, they were stopped by a striking woman with brown skin and midnight black hair that cascaded down her back. The woman smiled at Keith, draping her hand on his arm.

Karen stared, jealousy slicing through her as Keith and the stranger spoke in low voices. Feeling like an intruder, Karen began to step away.

"Karen, don't go." Keith's urgent tone took her by surprise. He then took her hand, glancing at the beautiful woman beside him. "This is Melanie Richards. She's one of the most awesome women you'll meet at this church." His voice filled with pride. "Melanie, this is Karen Brown, Ms. Doris's daughter."

Melanie shook Karen's hand. "It's so nice to meet you, Karen. How long will you be in town?"

"I–I'm not sure. I just needed to get away from Ocean City and spend some time with my mother."

Melanie's eyes widened. "Oh, well, I hope you have a nice visit." Somebody beckoned Melanie, so she left Karen and Keith to walk to the front of the sanctuary.

Keith led Karen to a seat, continuing to praise Melanie. "She's really a great woman. I don't know what the youth ministry would do without her." Was Keith interested in

Melanie romantically? She eyed Melanie. A few of the teens hugged her and it appeared she was well respected. Keith's deep voice filled with admiration as he spoke about her. Plus, both Keith and Melanie led the youth group together – they seemed to be the perfect couple. She eyed Keith again. Maybe she'd been misreading his signals. She'd sensed that he'd been at least a little bit interested in her...but, it was possible that she'd been wrong.

More teens arrived, filling the sanctuary with noise. When the band strummed the notes to a popular gospel song, the young people swayed, singing to the music. After the praise and worship, a few of the young people stepped forward, telling of recent battles they had been facing. Keith then stepped to the front of the stage, Melanie beside him, blatantly staring at him like a lovesick woman. Plus, she was so tall, slim and gorgeous. With her flawless brown skin and perfect features...well, she could imagine Keith being interested in Melanie.

Keith cleared his throat. "I just want all of you to remember never to give up. Most of you know what I went through as a teenager, and I want to remind you to stay focused on

God. Let Him lead you in your life."

As Melanie said a few words to the large group, Karen barely listened. Her mind was full of curiosity about Keith. . .his younger years. . .his family. . .his relationship with Melanie. She realized she knew so little about her mother's next-door neighbor, and she longed to find out more.

After Devo, a middle-aged woman approached Melanie and Keith, telling them that the pizzas had been delivered and were awaiting them downstairs. Karen assumed the woman was a church employee or a volunteer. After Keith made the appropriate announcement, the group trekked down to the basement. Melanie and Keith set the pizza boxes in a row on the long table, then set out plates, paper cups, napkins, a bucket of ice, and sodas. Watching them work together, Karen felt like a third wheel.

After Keith said grace, everybody got plates of food and broke up into groups to share the meal. Since Karen didn't know anybody, she sat at a table near the end and was surprised when Amanda sat beside her with her plate of pepperoni pizza and cup of orange soda.

Amanda smiled. "Hi, Karen."

"Hi, Amanda."

"I usually sit with my best friend Cassandra, but she's not here today."

"Oh. Well, thanks for joining me." Hopefully, they could get better acquainted. During Devo, amidst her negative thoughts concerning Keith and Melanie, she'd also thought about Amanda. Recalling what Keith had said about Amanda, she made a mental note to try not to say anything that might offend the teenager.

Karen bit into her pizza. The thick, spicy tomato sauce, melted cheese and salty pepperoni tasted amazing. She gobbled another bite. "This pizza is so good." She couldn't remember the last time she'd had pizza that tasted so delicious.

"Mr. Keith orders our pizza every week from the most popular Italian restaurant in the area."

She grinned as she enjoyed another bite of pizza. Figured Keith would order pizza from the best restaurant in town. He seemed to know a lot about food. She could imagine his owning his own restaurant. But, he'd told her that his calling was to become a preacher. Well, she'd need to remember to ask him about his divinity school search later.

She focused on the teenager sitting beside her. "So, Amanda, where do you live?"

As they feasted on pizza and sodas, Amanda told Karen about the neighborhood she lived in, how she'd been best friends with Cassandra since she'd entered high school, and about her impending eighteenth birthday. "I just wish God would open up the sky and money would pour into my lap."

"If that were to happen, what would you do?"

"I would buy myself a place to live. Then I wouldn't have to deal with crazy foster parents. I would take care of myself."

"Then what?"

"What do you mean?" The girl sipped her soda.

"If you were living alone, what would you do with yourself during the day? Would you want to go to college or get a job?"

The girl, attractive but wearing too much makeup, shook her head, looking at Karen as if she were crazy. "Oh no. You've got it all wrong. I wouldn't be living alone."

"Oh? You'd have a roommate?"

Amanda again gave Karen a befuddled look. "No, I'd have Ron with me."

Karen didn't like the way this conversation was playing out. "Who's Ron?"

"He's my boyfriend. We'd get married and then we'd live in the house together."

Karen inwardly groaned, finishing her pizza. "Well, Amanda, even if you were to marry Ron, it would still be a good idea for you to think about what you'd like to do for a living."

"Yeah, I guess you're right. Maybe I could get a job as a waitress." After a few bites of pizza, Amanda focused on Karen again. "What do you do for a living?"

Surprised, Karen began telling Amanda about being a hairdresser, winding up her shoptalk with, "One day maybe you could come down to the salon. I know they've been advertising for a shampoo girl."

"Okay, I might do that." Amanda nodded.

Sometime later, the teenagers assisted Melanie, Keith, and Karen with cleanup. Once the youth left, Karen again felt like a third wheel. Keith and Melanie stood in the corner. "Melanie, you need to go home and get some rest. You look exhausted. Have you been sleeping well?" The note of concern in his deep strong voice made her again question if he were involved with Melanie.

Melanie responded, but Karen couldn't hear what she said. The way they stood in the corner, away from Karen, made her feel as if they were hiding something. She narrowed her eyes and turned away from them. She folded her arms in front of her chest. No way did she want Keith to see her angry.

"Let, me walk you to your car." Keith made the offer to Melanie and Karen again swallowed her anger. She could see the church parking lot through the window. Keith walked Melanie to her car. They stood there, talking. Karen pulled out her phone to check the time. How long would they stand out there talking? Keith then hugged Melanie. Melanie then got into her car and drove away.

Ten whole minutes they were standing out there talking. What had they been talking about? Finally, Keith came strolling back to the church.

Keith checked to make sure everything was put away then locked the doors on their way out. He touched her shoulder. "Thanks so much for coming tonight."

"You're welcome. But I felt a little like a third wheel. I mean...Well, why did you need me when Melanie was here to help you?"

He raised his eyebrows, leading her to his vehicle. He opened her door before sliding into the driver's seat. "I wasn't sure if Melanie could come. I told you that she doesn't make it very often anymore." He started the engine. "This church is so blessed to have Melanie helping to lead the youth."

It rattled her that he kept praising Melanie. Didn't Keith realize that he had a gift in helping the youth, too? He wanted to be a pastor and seeing the way he acted with the youth this evening, she could imagine his fulfilling his dream of serving the lord as a minister. "You're a great youth leader, too. The kids really seem to look up to you. And it's obvious how much they like you."

"Yes, but it's nice to have an extra pair of hands." He played praise and worship music as he drove the short distance home. Gravel crunched when he pulled the car into his driveway. Cutting the ignition, he turned toward her. "Do you mind if we sit on my porch for a while?"

She nodded. It'd be good to spend some time alone with him. She really wanted to know if he had feelings for Melanie, but, she didn't want to appear jealous when she asked him about Melanie. She also wanted to know more about Keith. During Devo, he'd briefly mentioned going through a lot when he'd been a teen, so, she wondered what he'd been referring to. Soon, they sat on his porch, relaxing in lawn chairs. A gentle breeze blew and Karen tilted her head, relishing the wind kissing her skin.

"You know, Melanie was apprehensive about helping at first. But since she came on board, we've managed to increase the youth membership. In fact, it was her idea to have dinner after the service."

"Can the church afford to feed the teens each week?"

"The way they eat? No."

She laughed. "So, who pays for the pizza every Friday?"

"I do."

"Wow. That's generous of you." Keith really was a kind-hearted man, and that was one reason why she enjoyed spending time with him. She didn't want to talk about Melanie's youth pizza meal idea any longer. There was a more pressing subject she wanted to broach. So, she asked the question that had been burning in her mind since she'd met Melanie. "Keith. . . are—are the two of you dating?"

He jerked back. "Who, me and Melanie?"

Karen nodded.

"Of course not. Why do you ask?"

"Well, you keep singing her praises, s–so I just wondered. . ."

He grinned. "If I didn't know any better, I'd think you were jealous."

Karen's mouth dropped open. "Jealous? Me? You just keep talking about how great Melanie is, so I—I assumed...Well, never mind what I assumed." Feeling heat flare in her cheeks, Karen looked away for a few minutes, but her curiosity about Melanie soon got the better of her. Keith was right, she *had* been jealous. She supposed her reaction was a bit premature. Her and Keith had only spent a little bit of time together. She was attracted to him, but that was it. She figured she wanted to know the truth...well...she felt it was best to be honest. If Keith had a girlfriend, then she wanted to know about it. She turned back to face Keith. "So, Melanie joined the church after you did?"

"Yeah, I ran into her downtown one day. I hadn't talked to her since my father's funeral, and I told her about the new church

I'd joined."

"She came to your father's funeral?"

"Yeah, Melanie and I go way back. I've known her since I was a kid. We went to the same private school."

"I think she has feelings for you. You should have seen the way she was looking at you during Devo."

Keith scoffed. "Melanie's not interested in me. She's over that now."

Karen's heart skipped a beat. "What do you mean?"

"I took her to the prom in high school, and we used to hang out as friends. When I was about to go to college, she told me she'd always wished we could be more than friends. To tell you the truth, I was surprised she wanted to have anything to do with me romantically, considering my reputation."

"What reputation?"

He hesitated and sighed. "Well, I didn't have the best of reputations in high school. Anyway, I told her I'd always thought of her as a sister. My dad and her parents were so close, the idea of her being a girlfriend never entered my mind."

"What did she say when you told her how you felt?"

"She started crying. It was rough. I felt bad, but I thought she needed to know the truth."

"So, after that, you two kept in touch?"

"Yeah, when we went to college, we talked on the phone once in a while. We also texted. But the boyfriend-girlfriend thing was never brought up again, so I figured it wasn't an issue anymore."

"Was she a Christian back in high school?"

"No, she told me she got saved in college."

"I think she likes you."

Keith huffed. "You're a woman, so I'm surprised you didn't notice."

"Notice what?" Karen threw her hands up in the air, exasperated.

"Melanie's engagement ring."

Karen touched her finger, which no longer sported Lionel's ring. Bittersweet dreams of all she'd lost from her ex-fiancé's betrayal fluttered through her mind, but she pushed the recollections aside, focusing on their conversation. "Melanie's engaged?"

"She's been engaged for a few months. She's marrying a businessman named Duane. He owns a chain of restaurants in Maryland."

"Really? Which one?"

"The Blue Crab Grille."

"Wow. That's one of the most famous chains in Maryland. And Melanie is engaged to the owner?"

Keith nodded.

"Have you met him?"

"Yes. He seems to be a decent Christian man, and Melanie seems happy with him, most of the time, at least."

She mentally sighed with relief, knowing Keith was not involved with Melanie.

"I think it's kind of funny that you thought I was dating Melanie."

"Why?"

"Because I don't date." His deep voice rang with a note of finality.

Karen's heart sank. "You don't date? How come?"

A loud bark interrupted them. "Oh, I forgot to let Suzie out." He opened the screen door and the dog raced out, holding a leash in her mouth, her brown eyes pleading with Keith.

"I haven't taken Suzie out for a walk in days. I think she wants some exercise." He removed the leash from her mouth. "Want to come along?"

She chuckled, amused. "I could use the exercise, too."

"Great." He attached the leash to the dog's collar, and seconds later, they headed out of his gate. Streetlights shone on the sidewalk as they strolled through the neighborhood.

Karen was still curious about Keith's previous comment. "So why don't you date?" Breathless, she tried to keep up with Keith and Suzie's rapid pace. "Do—do you think you guys could slow down? Wha–what are we racing to? A fire?"

Keith smiled as Suzie dragged him toward a hydrant. "Well, maybe not a fire exactly." He pulled back on the leash. "Okay, Suzie, come on. Let's slow down." Once they'd reached an easier gait, he said, "The reason I don't date is because I'm not very good at relationships."

"You mean you've dated a lot in the past?"

They rounded a corner and passed another couple out walking their dog. Suzie greeted her fellow canine with a bark. "Suzie, be quiet." Keith continued, "I don't know if you'd call it dating. You see, I didn't accept Christ until I was almost out of grad school. My brother and I went to the same school as undergrads and, well, we had some pretty wild times."

"Are you talking about drinking, parties, stuff like that?"

"Yes, pretty much. I'm ashamed to say this, but when I was in high school and college, I slept with so many women that I can't even remember them all. Looking back at how irresponsible I was, I'm just glad I had enough sense to wear protection."

"You did all of this before you were saved?"

Suzie stopped at a large tree, sniffing the trunk. "Yes. You know, Karen, even though I was doing all of those things, I wasn't happy. My roommate, Steve, was a Christian, and he—"

"You and Kyle didn't share a dorm room?"

He shook his head. "No. We weren't roommates." He glanced at Suzie. "Anyway, Steve invited me to Bible study. I'd never really read the Bible much before, and I didn't think I would understand it." Suzie abandoned the tree, and they continued their stroll. "But once I'd started studying the Word, I found what was missing in my life." He paused a few seconds before continuing. "Remember the woman I told you about, the one who raised me and my brother?"

"Ms. Sonya?"

"Yes. She tried to share her faith with me and Kyle several times throughout the years, but we never listened. She asked my dad if we could go to church with her, and Kyle never wanted to go, but I went with her at least once a month."

"But. . .it didn't stick?"

"No, it didn't. I'm sorry to say I never even listened to the sermons. I mostly used church as another social outlet. I was so busy paying attention to the pretty women all dressed up that I didn't hear a word the pastor said. Once I got my driver's license, I had more freedom to go to the places I wanted, so I stopped going to church with her." He shook his head. "Ms. Sonya would fuss at us about our behavior. But after a while her lectures became like so much background noise."

"Your dad didn't know about your being gone all the time?"

"At the time, I didn't think he cared or even noticed."

Karen thought about his words for a while. "Since you never listened to Ms. Sonya about God, what prompted you to listen to your roommate?"

Keith sighed. "While I was in college, Ms. Sonya was in a car accident. At first, the doctors didn't think she was going to make it. She was in the hospital for weeks. During that time, I realized life could be cut short so suddenly, and I really wanted her to get better. I'd never been so depressed. When my roommate asked what was wrong, I told him about Ms. Sonya's accident and that I felt bad about never listening to what she said about God." Keith squeezed the leash as they continued to walk. "Steve said it was never too late to start studying God's Word, and that's when I started going to the Bible study on campus."

"Wow, it looks like you really went through a lot."

"Yeah. I'm just glad I finally made the right decision."

"So, is that why you're not close to your brother anymore? He doesn't understand your Christianity?"

He tensed. "I don't want to talk about my brother right now."

"O–okay, sorry." She paused. "But I still don't understand what all of this has to do with your decision not to date."

"Well, I told you that I was very

promiscuous."

"Yes?" She wasn't sure what to say about that.

"The attention I was able to get so easily from women. . ." He shook his head. "You know I got into some big trouble back then. I broke up a lot of relationships. Once I even slept with a married woman. And I'm ashamed of that."

She attempted to reason with him. "But you're a Christian now. Jesus has forgiven you."

"I know. But we should resist temptation. And I guess that's what I'm doing."

"I don't understand."

"When my college pastor studied the Word with me, he said new Christians needed to resist temptation, which for me meant avoiding women and romantic entanglements."

"When did you become a Christian?"

"I was twenty-four at the time. I started going to church and reading the Bible when I was an undergrad, but I didn't accept Christ until shortly before I received my MBA."

"You have an MBA?" She recalled his mentioning grad school, but, didn't realize he'd finished and had gotten a masters' degree.

"Don't sound so surprised."

"But you're a plumber."

"Tell me about it. My dad gave me grief about that for years. He said he didn't pay for my college education to throw it away on a blue-collar job."

"Why did you want to be a plumber?"

"I didn't want to sit in an office all day. I love going to different houses, driving around, fixing things."

She changed the subject. "So, you've been saved for six years? I'd hardly consider you a new Christian, and I don't think God would mind if you found a nice Christian woman to settle down with." They turned a corner, and he clutched the leash when Suzie saw another dog and tried to approach the animal.

"Suzie, calm down." The dog slowed and he continued speaking. "I don't trust myself. What if I get involved with somebody and revert back to my old womanizing ways? What if I get married and I find I wouldn't be a good husband? I don't want anybody to get their feelings hurt, and I'm not sure if I'm strong enough to be committed."

She imagined Keith would make a kind, loving husband.

"Since I've been involved with the church, I've found joy in ministering to the youth. I think the reason I have such affection for teens is because I remember what it's like to be young and confused." He looked at her. "Since I accepted Christ and cut out all romantic relationships, my life has been on track, and I don't want to mess up." He paused. "The Lord will probably change my mind, but right now I feel He's calling me to stay single and to work toward getting my degree at divinity school."

They finished the rest of their walk in silence, both lost in their own thoughts.

11

Over the next month, Karen continued assisting Keith with the youth on Fridays. The girls liked her. One night she gave a successful session on beauty tips. As Amanda and Karen grew closer together, Karen promised she'd help her find a job since the girl's high school graduation and eighteenth birthday were just around the corner.

Keith enjoyed spending time with Karen

and seeing her interact with the youth. As he continued praying about his relationship with Kyle, he imagined seeing his twin again, boasting about the beautiful woman who was slowly capturing his heart.

One day, Keith drove to Sandy Point State Park to enjoy a picnic with Ms. Sonya and her husband. He paid his entrance fee as the guard waved him through. After he parked, he pulled out his small cooler from the trunk. Although Ms. Sonya was providing the food for their picnic, she'd insisted that he bring some of his lemon chocolate buttercream candy for dessert. He'd made a fresh batch that morning and had placed it into the cooler with ice to prevent it from melting. The wind blew and the water appeared choppy. Fishing boats bobbed on the water and he noticed some crabbers in the distance. He found Ms. Sonya at the agreed-upon picnic area. He grinned as he approached her.

"Keith, it's been a long time since we've visited." Hearing her Jamaican accent filled him with pleasure. The petite woman's hair was now partially gray, but her dark face was wrinkle-free. She pulled him into a hug.

"It's good to see you again," he said once

they ended their embrace.

Her husband Terrance was just ending a phone call. He slid the phone into his pocket and joined them, his bald head shining in the late afternoon sun. "Keith, we haven't seen you in months. I'm glad you were able to come to our picnic today." The men shook hands.

Sonya's perceptive dark eyes pierced into Keith's. "I can tell something heavy is on your mind. Come on and sit down. The food is already laid out."

A white plastic tablecloth draped the picnic table. He plopped onto the picnic bench eyeing the beautiful beach before focusing on the food Ms. Sonya had prepared. He eyed the curried goat, fried plantains, and an assortment of other food. After they fixed their plates, Terrance blessed their meal. As they ate, Keith asked them about their two college-aged children, and Ms. Sonya and Terrance were more than happy to fill him in on all the details.

After lunch, Keith opened his cooler and removed the plastic container of candy. As they munched on their dessert, Ms. Sonya grinned. "Mind if I take the leftover candy home with me? Our kids will be visiting us next weekend and they've been craving your candy."

Keith chuckled. "Of course, you can take the candy home with you. It's the least I can do after that delicious meal you provided."

Terrance's phone buzzed. He checked the display. "I have to take this call. It's my job. I'm sorry Keith. I'm going to be on the phone for at least a half hour."

Keith shook his head. "Don't worry about it. I wanted to talk to Ms. Sonya about something anyway."

As Terrance focused on his call, Keith glanced at Ms. Sonya. "Do you mind if we take a walk on the beach? I wanted to talk to you about something."

"I'd love to walk with you on the beach Keith, but, we need to walk slowly. I'm not as young as you are and my knees hurt if I walk too fast." She smiled at him as they made their way toward the shore.

"Okay. I promise not to walk too fast. You can lead the way."

The wind whipped around them as the water crashed onto the sandy shore. Keith stopped sniffed. "Don't you just love the smell of the beach?"

"I sure do. It's so pretty and tranquil out

here. The water, the sand...the pretty sky." She slowly strolled the shoreline. Keith had to make himself walk at an extremely slow gait to accommodate his former nanny. "So, Keith, what's on your mind? I know you didn't want to come out here just to talk about how pretty it is at the beach."

Keith folded his arms in front of his chest. How could he begin? There was so much he wanted to tell Ms. Sonya. "I'm worried about something." He ran his fingers through his hair. "And I've been losing sleep over it."

"You know what the Lord says about worrying."

"I know, but I can't seem to help it."

"Has Kyle contacted you?"

Keith shook his head. "No, I haven't heard from him."

"If nothing's changed with your brother, what more is weighing you down?"

"Remember I told you about Ms. Doris, my next-door neighbor?"

"Yes, I remember. What about her?"

"Well, she has a daughter." Keith told her about Karen and how much he loved having her help with the teenagers. "I'd like to spend some time with her outside of the youth ministry."

"You want to date her?"

"Yes, but I'm not sure if that's a good idea."

"Why not? She's not married, is she?"

Keith scoffed. "No, but she came pretty close." He told of Lionel's deception and Karen's renewed faith, then said, "Ms. Sonya, I told you about how wild I was in college. I've never had a steady girlfriend. Me being with one woman, I don't know if that'll work."

"Keith, stop worrying about it so much. You've really grown as a Christian. I think if things work out with Karen, you would be okay."

"I don't know. Sometimes I wonder if she still has feelings for Lionel. With all of my doubts, maybe the Lord is trying to tell me not to pursue this relationship."

She stopped walking and touched his arm. "Or maybe He's telling you to pursue her, but to take it slow."

Keith squeezed Ms. Sonya's hand. "Maybe."

They continued walking in silence for a while. A couple strolled past them, holding hands. The couple stopped and shared a brief kiss. Just seeing the open affection reminded him about how much he wanted to kiss Karen.

"How is your divinity school search going?"

Glad for the change in subject, he told her about the colleges he was considering. "There's a place over near Virginia Beach that looks interesting. I'd like to go there for their open house this summer."

"When are you thinking of enrolling?"

"I'll probably start applying soon. Hopefully I can begin classes somewhere next fall, that's about a year and a half from now."

"Well, you should pray about that. And while you're at it, you should be praying about your situation with Karen. You know, honey, if you never let her know how you feel, you might regret it." She stopped walking and looked directly into his eyes. "Let me ask you something."

"Yes?"

"How would you feel if Karen started dating somebody else in your congregation?"

He'd noticed some of the men admiring her during Sunday services. Aaron always mentioned how classy Karen looked when she stepped into church every week. "It would bother me a lot if I saw Karen with another man." He then told her about Karen getting upset about his friendship with Melanie. "I think her reaction to my friendship with Melanie shows that she may be interested in going out with me."

"Well, I think you know what you need to do."

Keith spent the remainder of their stroll contemplating Sonya's advice. As he watched a fishing boat bobbing in the distance, he thought about what Karen would say if he asked her out on a real date.

12

Clutching a box of party decorations, Karen stepped into the private dining room of a family-style seafood restaurant. "Giving Amanda a surprise party was a great idea." She pulled a tablecloth out of the box.

Keith stood on a chair, hanging blue and white streamers on the wall. Sunlight splashed through the wide windows, lending the place a festive feel. He stepped down from the chair. "I wish there was more I could do for her."

"I'm worried about her, too. Hopefully, everything will work out."

"Yes, after asking around, I did find a couple who were willing to let Amanda stay with them at the end of the summer."

Karen placed the cloth over the table then turned to glance at Keith. "That's good news. I'm glad everybody's been praying for her."

Her eyes were drawn to his muscular calves, revealed by his knee-length shorts. She looked away. No way did she want to be caught staring. Since they'd been working together in the youth ministry over the last couple of months, she didn't think about Lionel as much as she used to. His deception still bothered her, but, her pain had originally been like a huge open wound, bleeding at the surface, smarting with pain. Now the wound had closed and was in the process of healing. She still felt a little pain, but, she felt with more time and a lot of prayer, Lionel would soon only be a bittersweet dream – a broken engagement from a man whom she'd once loved.

She pulled a gift from the shopping bag, placing it on the table. Turning, she caught

Keith staring at her. He smiled.

"What's so funny?"

He laughed. "Nothing. I was thinking how much you've changed since you moved back to Annapolis. Remember you didn't want to go back to church because of. . ." His smile faltered. "Well, you know what I'm talking about."

She knew, but she didn't want to ruin a nice day by talking about Lionel.

The door opened and some of the teenagers arrived.

"Hey, Karen," said Sharon, one of the youth, "I picked up the cake you ordered from the bakery." She glanced around the space, her curls gleaming in the sunlight. "Where should I put it?"

Karen nodded toward a table. "Right there is fine." Sharon opened the bakery box. The delicate roses and vines outlining the chocolate icing were beautiful. The words Happy Birthday, Amanda were scrolled across the triple-chocolate mousse cake. "Well, I hope Cassandra was right about chocolate being Amanda's favorite flavor."

They had barely finished setting up when Amanda arrived with one of the youth members. When she entered, everybody bellowed, "Surprise!"

"Oh, my goodness." Amanda smiled, tears streaming from her eyes. Karen looked closely at the girl. Thick makeup covered her pretty face. She frowned. Amanda never wore her makeup so thick. A few minutes later, she pulled her aside, shocked when she saw the shadow under her eye.

"What happened to your eye?" Karen touched the dark bruise. Looking away, Amanda didn't respond.

Karen's anger bubbled. "Did Ron hit you?"

Amanda frowned. "He didn't mean to."

Keith approached. "Is everything okay here?" He looked closely at Amanda's face then scowled. "What happened to your eye?"

Tears slid down Amanda's cheeks. "This is my birthday, and both of you are ruining it with your questions." She abandoned Keith and Karen, rejoining her party.

Karen touched his arm. "Keith, I don't know what to do. She says Ron didn't mean to hit her—"

He took her hand. "Honey, we'll talk to her another time."

"But Ron—"

He hugged her. "I know. We'll talk to her later."

Karen blinked away tears, saying a silent prayer for Amanda's well-being.

Soon the party was in full swing. As the teens filled up on an exorbitant amount of crab cakes and pasta, Karen's head rolled thinking about the bill Keith would be paying at the end of the evening.

Once the food and most of the cake had been eaten, the teens left the party. Amanda followed, grinning as she carried off her bundle of gifts. Karen still wished they could have talked about Ron, but she figured she would broach the subject again during their next Devo night. Right now, she was too exhausted to do anything.

Keith glanced at her. "Tired?"

"Very." Rubbing her eyes, she continued thinking about Amanda. "I hope Amanda's not seeing Ron today."

"I know. We can advise her, but we can't force her to break up with him."

"I know."

He stood and stretched. "It shouldn't take us long to clean up."

As they worked in companionable silence, Karen realized she could really get used to spending time with Keith. Being around him gave her a warm fuzzy feeling.

After they boxed up their stuff, they exited the private room, carrying their containers, and headed to the front of the restaurant. Karen nearly tripped when Keith's twin stumbled through the door. He looked at them, sneering.

"Well, if it isn't my little brother." Kyle stood on unstable feet, slouching toward them. She took a deep breath. It was unsettling to finally see Keith's twin brother in person while he was so drunk. Keith had once told her that Kyle often called him "little brother" since Kyle was born ten minutes before Keith. "If I'd known you were going to be here, I wouldn't have come."

Speechless, Karen leaned toward Keith as they set their boxes on a nearby table.

Placing his arm around Karen, Keith eyed his twin. "We were just leaving." He glanced around then turned back to his brother. "Are you here alone?"

Kyle's mouth hardened. "That's none of your business." His breath reeked of alcohol. Kyle looked at Karen. "Who's this?" He leered, and Karen jumped when Kyle clapped his hand on her shoulder.

Keith shoved his hand away. "Don't touch her."

" 'Don't touch her,' " Kyle mimicked his brother. "She's a pretty little thing." Kyle grinned. "Don't worry, little brother. I wouldn't try to steal your woman." He glared at Keith. "I don't steal things, unlike you."

Abandoning Karen, Keith forced Kyle outside. The day had turned overcast, and it looked like it was going to rain. While Keith stood outside with his brother, Karen watched them. Was it even possible for Keith to have a civilized conversation with Kyle since he was so sloshed?

An attractive woman exited the restroom, glancing around the restaurant.

She noticed the twins outside. "What in the world?" she mumbled.

"Are you here with Kyle?" Karen figured by the woman's surprised reaction from seeing the twins, that she was probably Kyle's date. She probably didn't know Kyle was a twin.

"What's it to you?" The woman gave her a cold look.

Okay, well, she'd only been trying to help. Maybe she shouldn't have said anything. She mentally shrugged. Maybe this woman was having a bad day. She glanced outside again. She could imagine the day being pretty awful if one were on a date with a man who was so sloshed. "I'm friends with his brother. Keith is concerned that Kyle might try to drive home drunk."

"I didn't even know he had a brother." She went outside and Karen followed. Keith spoke with Kyle's date for a few minutes. After Kyle and his date reentered the restaurant, Keith rejoined Karen. As thunder cracked from the cloudy sky, Keith frowned, his shoulders slumped. "Come on, let's go." They walked back into the restaurant to retrieve their boxes then headed out to Keith's vehicle.

They dumped the boxes into the car. Once they were both inside, Keith drove off as rain splattered against the windshield.

During their silent journey home, she stared at the swishing windshield wipers. Rain pelted the car like small angry bullets as another clap of thunder exploded in the gray, overcast sky. When he pulled into his driveway, he gripped the steering wheel.

Karen glanced over at him. "Do you want to talk about it?"

He sighed. His shoulders slumped. "I've been praying for my brother for the last nine months."

She remained silent, unsure of what to

say. The rain continued to pound against the window. "I'll start praying for your brother, too. Maybe with both of us praying, it'll make a difference."

"Sometimes I think it'll take a miracle to help him."

"Sometimes God does miracles. I'm sure you know that. Do you want me to go home?"

He held her hand. "Could we sit in the house for a while?"

She turned to look over at her mother's house, its windows dark. "Well, doesn't look like Mom's home. . .so sure. Why not?" She glanced around his car.

"What are you looking for?"

"Do you have an umbrella? I don't want to get my hair wet."

"No, but there's an old blanket in the back. You can cover your head with that." He reached over and found the tattered blanket and pressed it into her hands. Karen shielded her hair with the blanket as they bounded onto his porch. He unlocked the door and, after they'd stepped inside, turned on the lights.

Thunder cracked, prompting Suzie to bark. The lights flickered before they extinguished. Keith led her to the couch. "Sit down. I'm getting some candles." Soon after he lit the scented candles, the smells of vanilla and strawberry permeated the room. Suzie plodded into the living room and rested on the floor.

"I hope things work out with your brother."

He leaned back against the couch. "Thanks. That makes two of us."

"Do you see him often?"

"That was the first time I've spoken to him since the trial."

"What trial?"

"I already told you that my dad passed away."

"Yes..."

"Well, tonight you heard my brother say that I stole from him."

Karen nodded. "I assumed Kyle was talking crazy since he was drunk."

"Nope. He believes every word he said."

"Well, I know you didn't steal from your brother."

He folded his arms in front of his chest. "I didn't, but he doesn't see it that way."

"Okay, now I'm really confused. Do you want to clue me in?" "It's a long story."

Rain continued to batter against the

window. "I'm listening."

Keith began to explain, his voice sounding distant in the shadowy room. "After Kyle and I were in college, he decided he wanted to join my father in his law practice. Our dad wanted both of us to work with him, but I didn't want to be a lawyer." He shrugged. "After I'd gotten my bachelor's, I told my dad how I felt, and he wasn't pleased. Kyle was in law school, so my dad convinced me to get my MBA. While earning that, I got to know a lot of people in a local church. The pastor was a plumber. As a new Christian, I spent a lot of time with him and his family. I liked the idea of having my own business, and he showed me what to do to get started. My father was horrified when he found out."

She nodded.

"My dad said I brought shame to the family because I wanted to be a plumber. But he admired Kyle for joining the family law practice." His mouth set in a firm line. "I always felt my dad favored my brother over me because of his career choice." He frowned. "Anyway, sometime later, when I accepted Christ, I had to stop doing certain things. Kyle didn't get that. That's when things started getting tense between him and me."

He sighed, looking at her, the candlelight wavering in the darkness. "Then when my dad got sick with cancer, he couldn't work anymore. So, I moved in with him to help with his care." He took her hand. "I lived with my father for a year, sharing the gospel with him." He squeezed her hand. "I bonded with my dad. His cancer changed him."

"Did Kyle visit when your father was ill?"

He nodded. "Yes, but he didn't spend much time with him. I think seeing our father sick like that affected him. It—it was hard for him to be around Dad, knowing he was going to die. Kyle always did have a hard time dealing with death." He sighed. "Plus, he'd fallen in love and almost got engaged when my dad was sick."

"Really?"

"Yes. When Kyle started dating Andrea, I saw some changes in him. He was nicer, and their personalities seemed to click. Then he told me he was going to ask Andrea to marry him."

"What happened?"

"She left him for another man."

"He must've been devastated."

He nodded. "A few months later, our

father died. Kyle has been bitter ever since. That's when he started drinking more heavily." He paused for a few seconds. "When my dad's will was read, the *real* trouble started. Dad had gathered a lot of money over the years from his successful law practice and from some smart investments. He left me most of his wealth."

"You mentioned that to me when we had dinner."

"He only willed 15 percent of his estate to Kyle."

"Why such a small amount?"

"I don't know. I've asked myself that question a million times. It appears that he changed his will while I was living with him. Kyle thinks it was my doing, that I'd influenced Dad with my Christian talk. But I was as shocked as my brother when I heard Dad's will."

Karen shrugged. "If that's what's causing so much animosity between you two, then why don't you just give Kyle an amount equal to half the estate?"

"I wanted to, but not if my dad did this for a reason."

"Why didn't he tell you about this before he died?"

"I think he tried. The day before he passed, he said he had something important to discuss about his finances. But then the nurse gave him his medicine, and he—he just wanted to go to sleep."

"And never woke up?"

"Right." He stared at the candles. "After today's performance, it's obvious Kyle's drinking has gotten worse. He usually doesn't get so sloshed that early in the day. If he keeps this up, it'll affect his job."

"Earlier you mentioned a trial."

"Kyle took me to court, trying to prove I'd influenced Dad to change his will. But he lost the case. I don't blame him for being angry, but I'm still wondering why my father did this."

Walking home later that night, Karen thought about Keith's rocky relationship with his brother. Hopefully he'd find the answers to his questions soon so that he could heal the rift.

13

The following morning, Keith yawned while he dragged himself out of bed. Still yawning he ambled into his kitchen. Glancing out the window, he spotted Karen watering her mother's flowers.

The buds danced in the breeze as the moisture rushed from the hose. He studied her, unable to tear his eyes away. When she returned to her house, he roused himself from his reverie. Goodness, she was gorgeous. He sighed. He had to go and visit his brother this morning. He just had to try, yet again, to reason with his twin. He wished that he could take someone along for moral support.

Someone like Karen.

However, that wasn't possible. He liked Karen, plain and simple, and she'd already seen how ugly his brother could act while sloshed. This was something he needed to handle alone. Yesterday, it'd been nice to talk to her about his twin. He worried about Kyle and he knew that he needed to leave the whole ordeal in God's hands, let the Lord take care of it. But, he cared for his brother, and felt that he needed to do *something* to help him. He sighed again. *Time to wash up and get dressed.*

Minutes later, he pulled into the parking lot of his brother's trendy town house in an upscale Annapolis neighborhood. He knocked on the door, but when nobody answered, he used the spare key Kyle had given him years ago.

"Kyle!"

His brother stumbled down the stairs minutes later, his face still lazy with sleep.

"What are you doing here?"

"I came to talk to you."

Kyle shook his head. "Not now."

Keith sighed. "Man, I've been worried about you."

"My head hurts."

"Take some Tylenol. I'll make some coffee."

Several minutes later, the twins sat at the kitchen table. Kyle, having already downed two Tylenol with a cold glass of water, sat sipping his hot black coffee.

Keith looked at his brother. "Your eyes are red."

"So?"

"Do you remember running into me at the restaurant yesterday?"

Kyle winced. "Barely."

"What's up with you? You never get that drunk in the middle of the day." Kyle remained silent, sipping his coffee. "Kyle, you need help. And you know you don't have to walk this road alone."

Kyle shook his head. "Don't start talking to me about Jesus."

"Listen, part of your trouble is you're trying to handle all of your problems under your own power. You're still mad because Andrea left, you're still not over Dad's death—"

"Are you over his death?"

Keith shook his head. "No. But I take everything to the Lord, knowing He'll work everything out. That's what you need to do—lean on the Lord to help you with your problems."

"Some of my problems would be solved if you'd give me my half of the money."

"Kyle, I don't like it any better than you do. But Dad changed his will for a reason. And until I figure out why he arranged things the way he did, we're both stuck."

The brothers were silent as Kyle sipped his coffee. Kyle blinked, his eyes red and bleary. He focused on his brother. "Who was that woman with you at the restaurant?"

"What?" Keith was surprised Kyle even remembered seeing Karen.

"Are you deaf? I asked who you were with at the restaurant yesterday."

"Karen. And I don't like the way you talked to her. You can act pretty ugly when you're drunk."

Kyle hung his head. "I'm sorry about that," he mumbled. Lifting his head, he asked, "So what's up with you and this Karen?"

Keith frowned. "What do you mean?"

"I haven't seen you out with a woman since you turned religious. Are you two dating, engaged, or what?"

"She's my friend. Karen helps me with the youth ministry."

"That's it?" Kyle looked at Keith. "You like her. I can tell."

Keith shrugged. "So, what if I do?"

"I'm shocked. My brother has been living like a monk for six years, and now he's finally spending time with a woman."

Keith shrugged again. He didn't want to make a big deal out of this. He wasn't sure how Karen felt about him. "We're just friends for now. I'm not sure how she would feel about dating me."

Kyle stood, walked to the sink, and rinsed his mug. "My only advice to you is be careful. You know how I fell for Andrea. Days before I plan on asking her to marry me, she dumps me for another man. You'd better make sure Karen doesn't do that to you."

Keith knew Karen wouldn't be so callous, but he didn't think Kyle would understand, so he decided to change the subject. "I just stopped by to check up on you. You haven't talked to me since Dad died, and, well, I'm concerned about you. I want you to promise me you'll at least try to get some help. You could go to AA or something like that."

Kyle was silent as he placed his cup in the dishwasher.

Keith cleared his throat. "Is it okay if I call you once in a while to touch base?"

Kyle leaned against the counter, looking at his twin. "I guess, if that's what you want to do."

Keith inwardly cringed, still wishing there were more he could do to help his brother. At least Kyle had agreed to speak with him again, so it looked like the Lord had answered one of his prayers after all.

14

The alarm sounded, waking Keith from a deep sleep. Forcing his eyes open, he gazed at his clock, remembering he had set the alarm for 4:45 a.m. He lay back on his pillow, taking pleasure in knowing he was off from work today.

Eventually he got out of bed and, after a rough workout, showered then brushed his teeth. When he entered his kitchen, Suzie plodded over, begging for breakfast. "I'll feed you in a minute, girl." After starting a pot of coffee, he poured water and food into Suzie's dishes.

Hearing the water spurting from the hose at Ms. Doris's house, he opened the blinds in his kitchen and saw Karen outside, watering her mother's plants. Her slender arms held the hose over the flowers. She turned the faucet off and wrapped the hose around the stand. An idea formed in his head, and seconds later, he was approaching Karen in her mother's backyard.

"Hi there."

She jumped. "Oh, Keith. You scared me." She smiled. "What's up?"

He shrugged, still looking at her. Her hair was swept into a bun, a few curls dangling at the side. "You're off today, aren't you?"

"Yes, I am. Why?"

He relaxed against the oak tree. "If you don't have any plans, I was wondering if you wanted to take a ride with me today."

"A ride?"

"Yeah, remember I told you that I'm researching different divinity schools?"

She nodded.

"Well, I'm visiting a school over near

Virginia Beach. They're having an open house today. Do you want to come?"

"That's almost a four-hour drive."

He shrugged. "So? If we get started now, it won't be so bad. I've driven down there before in a day's time."

She paused and stared at the flowers for a few seconds. "You really want me to?"

"Yes, if you're not busy. I know it's last minute and all, but it didn't occur to me to ask you to come until this morning."

"What time are you leaving?"

"Soon. I was going to stop and have breakfast on the way. My treat. We can even spend some time on the beach after I visit the school. So—you interested?"

She grinned. "Yes, I'd like that. I promise I'll be ready soon."

He watched her as she headed back inside; then he returned to his own house, guzzled his coffee, and changed into slacks and a collared shirt. He then shoved swimming trunks, towel, and sunscreen into his gym bag. He placed his container of chocolate lemon buttercream candy, tuna pasta salad, fruit, and drinks into a cooler over ice. He figured they'd have a picnic lunch on the beach.

Minutes later, Karen met him in his driveway. She had a backpack and he assumed she'd brought her beach attire and a towel. The heavenly scent of her perfume enticed him as he opened the car door for her. After she stepped into the vehicle, he walked around to his side, got behind the wheel, and turned the radio to his favorite gospel station.

"What's in the cooler?"

"Lunch. If we have time, I was thinking we could sit on the beach and have something to eat."

"That sounds like a nice idea." Karen sighed. "I saw Melanie yesterday."

"Really? I heard she's been worshipping at her fiancé's church lately. How is she?"

"She came into the shop, asking me to give her a haircut."

Keith frowned. "Do you mean a short haircut?"

"Yes, and you know how long her hair is. It's so pretty, but I cut it like she wanted me to."

Keith shrugged. "Maybe she just needed a change."

"Well, after I cut her hair, she started crying, like she really hadn't wanted me to do it."

"That's strange."

"Yes. She said she messed up. Then she paid her bill and left the shop."

"That doesn't sound like Melanie. She's a tough woman who knows her own mind. I can't imagine her getting her hair cut like that unless she really wanted to. I think I'll call her soon to make sure she's okay."

"I still think she has feelings for you, Keith."

He huffed, wondering why Karen continued to think that Melanie had a crush on him. "You know that she's engaged. What more do you want me to say?"

Karen shrugged. "I saw the way she looked at you the few times she's shown up for Devo. Even though she's engaged, I don't think her feelings for you ever disappeared. And I've also noticed that you're very protective of her."

"Karen, I already explained that Melanie is like a sister to me. There's nothing romantic between us."

Karen changed the subject. "Have you heard from your brother?"

He stopped at a light. "I went to see him the day after Amanda's birthday party."

She grabbed his arm. "Why didn't you mention it to me? How is he doing?"

"Horrible. We talked a little bit, but I don't think he was very glad to see me."

"So, does this mean you're going to start talking to him again?"

"He told me that I could call him, but things are still strained between us. And I think they'll stay that way until I figure out why my father put me in charge of the inheritance."

The traffic slowed, and Keith glanced at the clock on his dashboard. "Do you have to be there at a certain time?" she asked him.

He nodded. "I'm supposed to meet the dean for an hour." He looked at the cars packed on the highway. He turned the radio to a traffic station and discovered there had been an accident farther ahead. "I think I'll be able to make it in time, but we won't be able to stop for breakfast."

The traffic continued to creep along, and almost an hour later they were going at a steady pace. Karen napped for part of the way. It was downright pleasant having her in the car with him during the long drive. Once they reached Virginia Beach, Keith had a mental tug-of-war – he wanted to stop and admire the beautiful beach, but, he was in a hurry. He checked the time. "I have to meet the dean in a half hour." He drove past the entrance to the college. The sign whizzed by, and seconds later he pulled into a 7-Eleven. "I'm going to run in here and get us something to eat."

He entered the store and soon returned with two sweet rolls and two containers of juice. Before they ate, he pulled out of the parking lot of the 7-Eleven and drove across the street to the college. He pulled into the parking lot outside the dean's office, where they feasted on the rolls and juice.

After finishing her breakfast and placing her trash into a bag, Karen tapped his shoulder. "If you're interviewing with the dean, I'm not sure you'll want me tagging along."

"I know what you mean. I guess 'interview' is kind of a strong word. It's really just a meeting to find out more about the school." He pulled a piece of paper out of his glove compartment. "I even have a list of questions that I need to ask him. I don't think it would be a problem if you come with me."

She shook her head. "That's okay." She glanced around the campus. "This is a small school."

Keith chuckled. "Yeah, I know. I'm not even sure if I'm going to enroll here. It's just one of many schools I'm checking out. Then I'll pray about it and see what God wants me to do."

A middle-aged man glanced at their car before strolling into the building. "That's the dean." Keith gestured toward the man.

"How do you know?"

"I saw his picture on the website." He glanced at his watch. "I'm supposed to meet with him in five minutes, so I'm going to head inside." He looked at her, feeling funny about leaving her sitting in the car. "I don't mind if you come inside with me."

She shook her head. "That's okay. Do you know how long you'll be?"

"They said the whole process should only take about an hour. He said it depended on how many questions I have."

She shrugged. "Take your time. I think I'll just walk around the campus and browse around the bookstore. I'll be back here in an hour. If you're not back, I'll wait."

"Okay." He handed her the car keys.

After his meeting with the dean was over and he'd had a tour around the campus, he returned to the car an hour and a half later and found Karen waiting. She was reading a novel, and she looked so pretty he could have just stared at her for hours.

She looked up and he smiled, trying to get his suddenly pounding heart to slow down. He approached the car and entered the vehicle. "What are you reading?"

She lifted the book for him to see. "It's a Christian romance novel."

"Is it a good story?"

She shrugged. "Pretty good."

He drove around the campus, showing her the different buildings and telling her about the tour he'd taken. When he was finished, he exited the campus.

"Where are we going now?" asked Karen.

"How about some lunch on the beach?"

After they'd found a place to change into their bathing suits, Keith snagged a parking spot close to the beach. Karen assisted him with carrying the cooler, beach chairs, and towels to the beach. The sun beamed onto the water. The waves tossed onto the sand while throngs of tourists strolled on the shore.

He grinned and held her and as they made themselves comfortable in their chairs. A warm breeze blew, kissing their skin. He glanced at Karen. She looked so pretty. Her lips were the color of dark cherries. *Lord, I want to ask Karen if she'll date me.* He closed his eyes.

"It sure feels nice out here." Karen's voice, sweet as honey, interrupted his musings. Tonight. He'd ask her about...well...about their dating after he'd taken her home tonight. Yes, that's what he'd do.

He breathed deeply as some birds swooped onto the shore, seeking stray crumbs of bread. It was a perfect day. It wasn't too hot or too cold, and he was having a great time just being alone with Karen. He released her hand and opened the cooler. Again, he reminisced about the way Karen had reacted when she'd tasted his cooking for the first time. She'd loved his omelet and his candy. He'd often received compliments on his tuna pasta salad, so, he hoped she enjoyed it.

He again took Karen's small hand and bowed his head. "Lord, thank You for this beautiful day and for providing us with this wonderful meal." He paused, squeezing her fingers. "And, Lord, thank You for allowing me to spend the day with my friend Karen.

Amen."

Karen squeezed his hand. "Amen."

"That looks good." She eyed the tuna salad. "I'm so hungry."

He grinned as he handed her a napkin and a plastic spoon and a container of tuna pasta salad. He opened their sodas as she sampled his tuna salad. "Keith, this tuna pasta salad is amazing."

He laughed, pleased that she was enjoying the meal. The wind whipped around them as they enjoyed their food.

Karen grinned. "You ever notice how the beach smells? It's so clean and refreshing." She then shoved another bite of tuna salad into her mouth.

He sniffed. The beach had a nice, briny odor. "Yeah, I know what you mean." With the sun beaming down on them, the birds swooping through the sky, the waves tossing onto the sand...well...this day just couldn't get any more perfect.

They took a long stroll along the edge of the water. Later, they went into the water together. He'd brought a beach ball and they playfully tossed it back and forth. When they took a break, they enjoyed the chocolate lemon buttercreams he'd brought for their dessert.

After they'd finished their dessert, Karen sighed. "I'm going over there to the restroom. I'll be back in a few minutes."

"Take your time." Such a wonderful day. He gathered their trash and placing it into the bin. He then plopped back into his beach chair. He sighed before closing his eyes. "Lord, I'm falling for Karen and I don't know what to do about it. I'm not sure if I should tell her how I feel." He paused for a few seconds. "Please guide me in saying the right words to her, Lord. Amen."

He opened his eyes, delighting in the warm weather. Minutes later, Karen approached, giving him a small smile.

"Are you okay?" she asked.

His heart nearly flopped when he heard the note of concern in her pretty voice. "Why do you ask?"

She shrugged. "You look a little worried."

When she sat beside him, he smiled, taking her small hand into his. He struggled with trying to find the right words to tell her his feelings, but decided he would wait until they returned to his house. "I'm fine. Just relaxing."

"Are you ready to go home? We've got a

long drive."

If it were up to him, he'd sit out here with Karen all evening. He checked his watch. "Not really. Actually, I've got another surprise. Remember I told you about my old college roommate, Steve?"

"Yes?"

"Well, we pass by his town on our way home. I told him I'd stop by and visit today. We don't have to stay for long."

She grinned. "Keith that sounds nice. Except for church, I've never met any of your friends."

They found a public place to shower and change back into their clothes before the long drive back.

15

When Keith pulled into Steve's driveway, a man rushed out to the car. "Keith! What's up, man?"

Keith laughed, exiting the car. The men shared a brief hug and a hearty handshake. "Nothing much. Just came from checking out a Bible college."

Steve glanced inside the car, seeing Karen for the first time. "You brought somebody with you?"

Karen stepped out of the vehicle, amused by Steve's jovial nature. "I'm Karen."

"Pleased to meet you, Karen." Steve squeezed her hand before pulling her into a brief hug. He gazed at her with his warm brown eyes. "Keith! She's beautiful." Steve gave Karen a playful wink. "Where in the world have you been hiding her?"

A short woman, her belly swollen with child, stepped through the front door. "Steve, aren't you going to invite your friends inside?" Exasperation tinged her voice, but her smile was bright like the sun.

The group strolled into the house. Keith pulled the pregnant woman into a hug. "You look like you're about to deliver, Dianne!" The young woman laughed, swatting Keith on the arm.

After the women were introduced, Keith sat in the living room with Steve, telling him about his divinity school visit.

While the men were engrossed in conversation, Dianne whisked Karen into the kitchen. "Please, Karen, have a seat. Would you like anything to eat or drink?"

"We were eating all day, so I'm stuffed, but thanks for asking." Karen glanced at

Dianne's stomach. "When are you due?"

Dianne chuckled. "Tomorrow."

Karen gasped. "No way! Really?"

"Yeah, really!"

Mesmerized, Karen watched Dianne's stomach move. "Can I touch?"

"Sure!" Dianne took Karen's hand, placing it over her belly.

Karen laughed, feeling a solid kick to her palm. "That was hard."

"Yeah, he's a strong little guy." She poured a glass of milk then joined Karen at the table. "So, do you have any children, Karen?"

"No, but I'd like to someday, if I ever find the right person to settle down with." She toyed with the strap of her purse. "Monica, one of my best friends, just had a baby. I haven't had a chance to visit her in Ocean City since the baby was born, but I can't wait to see her *and* her new little girl."

The two women sat in silence for a few minutes before Dianne spoke. "So, you're Keith's next-door neighbor?"

Karen nodded. "That's right. A few months ago, I moved from Ocean City back home to my mother's house in Annapolis, right next door to Keith. He and my mother are friends and worship at the same church."

"It appears you and Keith became friends, too."

"Yes, we work together in the youth ministry at the church."

Dianne sipped her milk. "Well, you can be honest with me. I know that the two of you are more than just friends."

Karen frowned. "Not really."

"You don't like him?"

Karen suddenly felt like she was fourteen again, gossiping at a slumber party with a girlfriend. She glanced toward the living room, not wanting the men to overhear.

Dianne waved toward the other room. "They're not paying us any attention. When Steve and Keith get together, they talk forever."

"What do they talk about?"

"Everything! The Bible, churches, sports, problems, you name it. I'll bet Keith said you guys weren't going to stay long, didn't he?"

Surprised, Karen responded, "Yes, he did."

"Well, if I know those two, you'll be fortunate if you get home before midnight."

"You're kidding."

"Nope." She took another sip of milk. "So, do you like Keith?"

Chuckling, Karen evaded answering by asking a question of her own. "How old are you, Dianne?"

"I'm twenty-three. Steve's thirty, but our age difference doesn't bother me."

"Is this your first child?"

"Yes, and I'm so excited!" She finished her drink, placing the glass into the sink. "Would you like to see our nursery?"

"Sure."

Dianne chatted all the way up the stairs. She then opened the door, and a profusion of blue, green, and yellow surrounded the space, enveloping the room with warmth. "Look at this!" Dianne said, grinning as she stepped over to the cherrywood crib, then turned the knob on a mobile. Soon a lullaby filled the room, and animals twirled in a circle, in tune with the music.

"It's lovely, Dianne."

"Thanks. We're having a boy, but I didn't want the room to be all blue. That's why I made it blue, green, and yellow."

Karen continued to relish the nursery, admiring the animals and cartoon characters stenciled on the wall.

Dianne interrupted her thoughts. "So, what's up with you and Keith Baxter?"

Karen laughed, immediately liking Dianne's easygoing personality, in spite of her persistent curiosity. "I told you, we're friends."

"Just friends?"

"Yes, we're just friends."

"Don't you like him?"

"He's nice," Karen admitted.

"Don't you think he's cute?"

"Dianne!"

"Well, he is! Don't get me wrong, Steve is my number one man, but at my wedding. . ."

When Dianne didn't continue, Karen's own curiosity was aroused. "What about your wedding?"

"Keith was Steve's best man at our wedding two and a half years ago. Every unmarried woman in my bridal party wanted his phone number. Keith got hit on so many times that I felt sorry for him." The mobile stopped, so Dianne turned the knob again, continuing to speak. "The whole time I've known Keith, he's never brought anybody over to meet us. He always comes alone and never mentions that he's dating anybody. Do you know if he's still having issues with his brother?"

Karen nodded. "They still have some

things unresolved. Keith did go to visit Kyle recently, so at least they're speaking a little bit."

Dianne looked away. "That's so sad. I wish they would just make up. Steve told me that Keith's rift with his brother really breaks his heart."

"Yes, it does."

She beckoned Karen out of the room. "Come on. I want to show you our wedding album. You can see what Keith looks like in a tux!"

Karen smiled as she followed the waddling woman to a room down the hall. After they'd gone through the wedding album, Dianne shared photos of her family, telling funny stories about things that had happened when she was a little girl. One childhood anecdote caused Karen to laugh so hard that tears rolled down her cheeks.

"Dianne, what in the world are you women doing up here? You sound like you're having too good of a time," commented Steve.

Keith entered behind his friend. "I don't think I've ever seen you laugh so hard, Karen."

"What are you two talking about?" asked Steve.

Dianne raised her eyebrows. "Just a little girl talk. I'll bet the only reason you guys came up here is because you're hungry."

Karen glanced at her watch, shocked that so much time had passed. Her stomach rumbled with hunger, reminding her that it had been hours since they'd eaten.

Steve playfully hugged his wife. "I'm ready for some grub!"

The foursome climbed down the stairs and entered the kitchen. Dianne opened the freezer and pulled out a package of frozen hamburger patties. "We were going to have hamburgers and chips for dinner. These patties will cook up in a few minutes on our electric grill."

Karen helped Dianne fix dinner. Soon they'd grilled the meat and served up burgers and chips for everyone. Steve took Dianne's hand. "I'll bless the table before we eat," he announced. Everyone bowed their heads and joined hands. Steve's strong voice soon filled the kitchen. "Lord, thank You for this wonderful day and for the blessing of having friends like Keith and Karen. And, Lord, please be with Dianne. Let your Holy Spirit protect her as we get closer to the time of our baby's birth. Amen."

"Amen," everybody mumbled.

Steve clapped his hands. "Now I'm ready to eat!"

Karen delighted in the fabulous fare and the friendly conversation at the table. Before she knew it, it was late and Keith suggested they head home. Both Dianne and Steve pulled Karen into a hug.

Dianne gave Karen a wide smile. "I want you to come back and visit us again. I had a good time today."

"Thanks, Dianne. I had a good time, too. Maybe I can ride over when Keith comes back to visit."

Shaking Keith's hand, Steve said, "Listen, buddy, don't keep Karen all to yourself anymore. Be sure to bring her by sometime after the baby is born."

Keith chuckled as he wrapped Steve up in a bear hug, saying, "We'll come back to visit soon."

While Keith drove away from the house, Karen waved to his friends standing in the driveway.

16

As he pulled into his driveway late that night, Keith glanced at Karen. Oh, what a perfect day. Now, he just needed to talk to her, tell her what he'd been thinking all day. She was bound to know that he liked her, after all, he'd asked to spend the entire day with her. He'd been proud to introduce her to Steve and Dianne. *Maybe I should ask her now...*

They exited the car and he looked up,

amazed at the brilliant stars in the heavens. The stars twinkled a bit brighter this evening. They stood in front of his car, observing the sky.

Karen smiled at him and stifled a yawn. It was past midnight, so, he figured she was tired. "Keith, it's so pretty tonight."

"Yes, it is."

"I had a great time. I especially loved meeting Steve and Dianne."

Lord, let me say the right things. He pulled Karen into his arms. "Maybe we can drive down another time and visit again. I'm sure Dianne would like you to see her baby."

He released her, taking her hands. "Keith—"

"Karen—"

She chuckled, and their eyes met. "Well, Karen, looks like both of us have something to say."

"Why don't you go first?"

Grinning, he squeezed her fingers, wanting to share his feelings. "Well, I—"

"Karen!"

Doris Brown's voice carried across the yard, and Keith winced. *Talk about bad timing.*

"Mom, what is it?"

As Doris hurried over to Keith's driveway, wearing her pajamas and bathrobe, he dropped Karen's hands then stepped away, his euphoric mood shattered.

Doris approached Karen. "Honey, there's an important message for you. You forgot your phone so I couldn't reach you."

"Oh, my goodness, I forgot my phone. I didn't even realize…"

Keith cleared his throat. "You could've called my phone Ms. Doris."

Ms. Doris shook her head. "Keith, I don't have your cell phone number."

"You don't?"

She shook her head. "Whenever I've needed you, I just drop by your house. You never got around to sharing your number with me."

Karen grabbed her mother's arm. "Enough talking about phone numbers. What's wrong? Did something happen to Monica or Anna?"

Doris shook her head. "No, nothing like that. But Monica phoned about ten minutes ago. Karen, she says Lionel turned himself in to the police last week. He's already had a hearing and…he's in jail."

Karen took a deep breath, pressed her

hand across her quivering mouth. "Are you sure?"

Goodness, she was upset. That snake Lionel...Karen had been having a great time all day, he was sure of it, and now her ex-fiancé had to go and louse up the best day he'd had in...well...in a good long while. He mentally sighed. He just needed Karen to know he'd be there for her. Her mom looked upset, too, so, it wouldn't surprise him if the two of them wanted to talk about this alone.

Ms. Doris nodded. "Monica claims they won't issue bail for him since he disappeared before his first hearing." She touched her daughter's face. "You might want to call Monica back."

Karen broke away from her mother and hurried over to her house.

Keith couldn't help himself. He had to find out if Karen still had feelings for Lionel. He followed the two women into Ms. Doris's home.

Karen grabbed her phone from the kitchen table and speed dialed Monica's phone number. Monica answered on the first ring.

"Monica, it's Karen. What's happened? Lionel turned himself in?"

"Yes. Both he and Michelle. Last week—"

"Last week? Why didn't you call me then?"

"I wasn't sure if I should. I know he hurt you a lot, and Anna and I struggled with telling you."

Karen rolled her eyes. "Monica, I'm a grown woman. You and Anna don't have to protect me. So where has Lionel been all this time?"

"I'm not sure. But he's back and in jail. He hasn't had his trial yet, only the hearing."

"I have to see him. Is he allowed to have visitors?"

"As far as I know, yes." A baby's cry carried over the wire. Monica sighed. "Karen, I have to go. Mica is hungry. You might want to think and pray about seeing Lionel again. Make sure this is what you want to do. Your mother told me you're involved with somebody else now—"

"No. I—I am not."

"But she said—"

"I don't care what she said. It's not true. Keith and I are. . .just friends, that's all." Karen clutched the phone, her thoughts reeling. The baby cried again.

"Listen, I've really gotta go. Call me later if you want to talk." With that, Monica hung up the phone.

Karen continued holding the phone then turned toward her mother. "I'm going to Ocean City tomorrow."

"I can't believe it. You're going down there to see him?" Keith's deep voice thundered through the kitchen.

Karen dropped the phone onto the kitchen table, turning toward him in surprise. "What are *you* doing here?" If she'd known he'd been standing in her kitchen, she wouldn't have told Monica about their being just friends.

"I followed you. I—I had to know. . ."

Her mother touched her arm. "Honey, are you sure this is what you want to do?"

Karen huffed, staring at her mother's face etched with concern. And at Keith, whose lips were set in a hard line and eyes sparkled with anger. Didn't they understand why she needed to do this?

"I'm going to Ocean City tomorrow, and that's final. I'll just call the salon and ask Deidre and Sheronda to cover for me."

Keith folded his arms in front of his chest.

"I don't think you should go."

Karen glared at him. "And I don't think *you* should be telling me what to do."

His mouth dropped open. An instant later he turned on his heels and strode from the kitchen, the screen door banging shut behind him.

Karen watched him storm back to his house. "What's his problem?" She needed to bring closure to her relationship with Lionel. Why couldn't he understand that?

Her mother sat at the table. "Honey, don't you realize that Keith is falling for you?"

She grunted. "Mom, you're letting your imagination run wild."

"Why do you say that?"

She shrugged. "Well, Keith and I have a good time together, but that's all it is. Besides, right now he's focusing on finding the right divinity school and fixing his relationship with his brother. On top of that, he's already told me he doesn't date." She kept the fact of Keith's promiscuous past to herself, not sure it was hers to share.

"Karen, you just *went* on a date with Keith—today."

"Today's outing was not a date. He just wanted somebody to ride with him to

Virginia Beach to see the college. And frankly, Mom, I don't want to talk about this right now. My mind is on other things."

"There's nothing more you can do tonight about tomorrow's visit to Lionel. But you *can* come here, sit down, and tell me what you two did today." She patted the empty chair beside her.

Resigned, Karen sighed and plopped down. "Mom, really, I don't want—"

"Just talk to me. It'll keep your mind off other things, help calm your nerves."

"Yeah, okay, whatever." Karen took another deep, calming breath. "When I was watering your flowers this morning, Keith came over and asked me to go to the Bible college with him." She shrugged. "I didn't have any plans, so I went. You got the note I left you, right?"

"Yes. So, what did the two of you do?"

Karen struggled to sort her scrambling thoughts. *Lord, give me peace and patience.* "It was no big deal. We went to the campus and Keith interviewed with the dean. Afterward, we spent the day on the beach and we ate the lunch and the candy he'd fixed for us." Fiddling with the salt and pepper shakers on the table, she continued to tell about her day. "I met Keith's college roommate Steve and his wife, Dianne. They're so much fun, and they're friendly, too. I'd like to visit them again sometime after Dianne has her baby." She gazed at her mother. "We ate dinner with Steve and Dianne; then we drove home. And that's all there was to it."

Her mother smiled. "Karen, Keith has feelings for you, but you're just having a hard time seeing that. I mean, you go on this road trip together for the day, and then he introduces you to his friends. It's obvious he likes being with you and was anxious for you to meet Steve and Dianne."

Karen shook her head. "Mom, he just wanted to have some company today, that's all." She thought back to her and Keith's previous conversations. "He just wants to be there for me like a friend, to help me get over Lionel."

"Well, I don't know what else I can say to convince you. But that man is falling for you. And whether you realize it or not, I think you're falling for him."

Karen sighed, ignoring her mother's observations. Well, maybe she shouldn't have lashed out at Keith. Had she hurt his feelings? What could she do to make him feel better? "Maybe I overreacted earlier. Maybe I shouldn't have yelled at him. It's just that after that phone conversation with Monica. . .I can't seem to think straight." She glanced through the kitchen window, noting that the lights in Keith's house were on. "Do you think I should go over and apologize?"

Her mom shook her head. "No. Give him some time to cool off. Maybe you can talk to him in the morning. Both of you seem to be early risers."

Her mother stood and stretched. "Well, I'm going to get ready for bed. You should go to bed, too. You've got a big day tomorrow." When her comment was met with silence, she squeezed her daughter's shoulder. "Good night, pumpkin. Don't stay up too late."

After her mom left the kitchen, Karen sighed, staring at the ceiling. The brief conversation she'd had with her mother about Keith made her temporarily forget about her planned mission: to go to Ocean City and visit Lionel Adams, desperate to find the answers to the questions that plagued her. She prayed, "Lord, please be with me. Give me wisdom and courage for tomorrow. And if there's any sleep to be had tonight, please help me find it. Amen."

17

The entire night, Karen tossed and turned as she mentally relived the horrid day when she'd found out about Lionel's crime against their church. Between short, pleading prayers for direction and healing, snatches of bittersweet dreams wove through her mind - the days Lionel courted her and the day he asked her to marry him. How loving and caring he'd been when she'd grieved over her father's death. His sweetness, tenderness - all the traits that had caused her to fall in love with him.

When the rays of the early morning sun began to lighten her room, she sat up in bed, rubbing her eyes with a tired sigh. Fatigue washed through her body, but there wasn't anything she could do about it now. She was too wired up to sleep, and she wondered if she was strong enough to drive the two and a half hours to Ocean City.

She finally pulled herself out of bed then washed and got dressed. When she opened the door to the backyard, ready to water her mother's flowers, she saw Keith standing on his porch, looking at her. He remained silent as he climbed down his steps and walked over to her house. His brown eyes had softened from the previous night, and his mouth drooped as he placed his hand on her shoulder. "Are you okay? You have circles under your eyes."

"I—I didn't sleep very well." His hand felt downright nice, resting on her shoulder. There was just something comforting about his touching her when she felt bad. She guessed it was because he cared and she figured he'd offer his support if she needed it. She sniffed. He smelled delicious, just like lemons and chocolate. He'd probably gotten up early to make a batch of candy. Perhaps his making candy helped him to deal with…well…whatever he was dealing with.

"Look, I'm sorry for losing my temper last night."

"I'm sorry for yelling at you, too, Keith."

"I was just trying to protect you from. . ." He squeezed her shoulder. "Karen, I—I don't think you should visit Lionel."

She sighed. "Keith, this is something that I have to do."

"Why?" His voice softened and his eyes pleaded with her.

"I have to try to put this whole thing behind me and seeing Lionel will help me to do that."

"Is he allowed to have visitors?"

"Monica says she thinks so."

He removed his hand from her shoulder, looking away. "When are you leaving?"

"This morning."

"I don't want you driving down there by yourself." His authoritative tone surprised her. "You still look half asleep. Are you sure you're up to the trip?"

"I can make it down there just fine. If I get too tired, I'll stop and rest."

"You sure are stubborn." He hesitated. "Listen, can you wait a few hours before you leave? I'd like to come with you." He glanced at his watch. "I have to fix somebody's toilet early this morning; then I'll have to call George, a colleague of mine. He can handle the rest of today's jobs for me."

Her mouth dropped open. "I don't want you rearranging your whole schedule because of me. You have a business to run."

He nodded. "That's true, but I have to make sure you're okay, too."

"I'm not your responsibility."

"I know you're not, but. . ." He sighed, his eyes scanning the houses lining their street. "Karen, there's something you should know."

She frowned. "What?"

"Last night, before your mother interrupted us, I was going to tell you that I had a great time with you yesterday."

"I had a good time, too."

He sighed. "Well, I wanted to know if you'd be open to the idea of spending more time with me, out–outside of doing the youth ministry." He paused. "I like you, Karen, and

I. . .I care about you." His voice turned gruff. "I can't bear to see you get hurt. Please. Don't go to see Lionel." He took a deep breath.

Karen's heart skipped a beat. She didn't know what to say.

When she remained silent, he rushed on. "You don't have to tell me what you think about my idea right now. I know you've got a lot on your mind. But once you have everything sorted out, I'd like you to think about what I'm asking you."

She nodded. "I will. I promise. But right now I have to go to Ocean City." She paced the small yard in silence, gathering her thoughts as pansies, marigolds, and roses swayed in the warm breeze. She took a deep breath. "I was engaged to Lionel. I was in love with him."

Keith winced.

She hurried on. "I—I need to talk to him, find out why he proposed to me and then apparently had an affair with somebody else."

"He's a loser, Karen. That's why. Men do that all the time." He stepped toward her, taking her hand.

Warmth traveled up her arm from his

touch. She closed her eyes, enjoying his chocolatey-lemon smell. Heaven help her, she wanted Keith to hug her and tell her everything would be okay. She wanted to enjoy the warmth and comfort from his touch. She wanted to just sit with him all day, in his kitchen, feasting on candy while they talked. Yesterday had been wonderful, but...even if she could find some happiness with Keith, she knew that she'd always wonder about Lionel's reasons for acting the way that he had. She needed to at least *try* to talk to her ex-fiancé.

"Karen, nobody knows better than I do how irresponsible some men can be. But, you and me. That's something special. If you'll just give me a chance, I guarantee I'll do my best to treat you the way you deserve."

Mere inches separated them. Keith's head leaned in closer to hers but then stopped. Staring into her eyes, he brushed his finger against her cheek, a gesture as sweet and endearing as a kiss.

Karen took a few steps away, removing her hand from his. "I—I have to go."

"Let me ask you something. If Lionel had disappeared forever, not to be found, do you think you'd ever be able to put this whole thing behind you and move on?"

She gritted her teeth. "That's not a fair question."

"Why not?"

"Because Lionel *hasn't* disappeared. So that point is moot. But there's one thing you haven't even considered. Have you even thought about the fact that maybe God wants me to do this?"

"What?"

"Maybe God moved Lionel to turn himself in and allowed me to find out about it so that I can go confront him and get some answers."

"Maybe," Keith mumbled, but the future pastor sounded doubtful.

"Well, let me ask you something else."

He nodded towards her. "Go ahead."

"If you had a member of your church with my problem, how would you advise her?"

He frowned, his brown eyes crinkled with confusion. "What do you mean?"

She threw her hands up in the air. "I mean what I just said. Pretend you're pastoring a church, and one of the members comes to you with this problem. Her fiancé has disappeared with the church's funds. It's rumored he's had an affair with the assistant treasurer who's also disappeared. He's turned himself in and is now in custody. She wants to go and visit him. Would you advise this person *not* to see her ex-fiancé?"

He turned away, running his fingers over his short hair. He finally turned back toward her. "I would tell her to pray about it and do as she felt led."

She touched his arm, wishing she could wipe the sullen expression from his beautiful face. "Keith, I've done that. I spent part of the night reminiscing about the time I've spent with Lionel, and another part seeking God's will. I feel led to do this, Keith, but when you get angry and upset with me, I feel like you're interfering with God's plan for my life."

"I don't mean to make you feel that way. If I do, then I'm sorry." She nodded, accepting his apology.

"Will you at least let me take you to Ocean City? I don't think you should be going down there by yourself." He glanced at his watch. "Just give me a couple of hours to get everything together with my clients, and then I'll pick you up."

She was touched that Keith insisted on coming with her, even though he didn't approve of her decision. "Okay, that's fine.

To tell you the truth, it'll be nice having someone else do the driving." She tried to stifle a yawn.

He checked his watch again, and they agreed to meet in a few hours.

18

When Keith returned to his house, he called George, his friend in the business who handled his workload when he needed to take time off. Then he left to do the repair at his client's house.

Returning home, he was happy to see Karen sitting on his porch, waiting for him.

"Are you ready?" She gripped the strap of her purse when she asked the question.

I'll never be ready to take you to see another man. Brushing that thought aside, he focused on her. "Let me just get out of these work clothes and wash up a bit. Then we can get going. I'll only be a minute."

After he'd cleaned up he opened the refrigerator and removed the glass bowl of his chocolate lemon buttercreams. The screen door banged shut as Karen came into the kitchen. She eyed the candy and swiped a piece. She bit into the candy. "Eating your candy makes me feel so much better. If I'd had some last night, I'd have eaten a dozen pieces." She took another bite.

Even though she still chewed, he touched her cheek. She stopped chewing and looked directly into his eyes. Her eyes were a dark, rich, brown, just like the chocolate he used to make his candy. Chocolate dotted the side of her mouth so he took a napkin and carefully wiped the chocolate from her face. Caught off-guard by the strong feelings churning through him, he took a deep breath and focused on the candy.

"I thought I'd take this candy over to your friends' house. I've never met them but...well..." He took another deep breath. "I want them to like me." Would they immediately be suspicious of him and compare him to Lionel? Did Karen have a track record of dating losers?

He removed a plastic container from the cupboard and dropped the candies into the container. He then took his small cooler and filled it with ice. He placed the candy on top of the ice. He figured if they didn't get a chance to eat the candy for some reason, he could always leave it with Monica and....what was the other woman's name? Anna, that was it. He could leave the candy for them to enjoy later.

"It's nice of you to take the candy to my friends. I think they'll like it, especially Anna." Nice to hear that she appreciated his small gesture.

When they were finally settled into his car and had buckled their seat belts, he pulled out of his driveway. Once on the highway, he worked up the nerve to ask her a question that had been burning in his mind like hot fire. "When we get to Ocean City, where do you want to head first—to see your friends...or Lionel?"

When his question was met with silence, he glanced at Karen and noticed she was fast asleep. The urge to kiss her cheek and cover her with a light blanket flowed through him, reminding him how his feelings for Karen had grown in such a short time.

Hours later, when they entered Ocean City, Karen sat up blinking, looking around. "I can't believe I slept the whole way here."

"You were tired. You needed it." He pulled onto the main road. "Fortunately, you woke up just in time. From this point on, you'll need to give me some directions. Where are we headed first?" He couldn't bring himself to ask where the jail was located.

"I called Monica and Anna this morning. They said they would meet me over at Monica's house."

He swallowed, still wondering how this whole thing was going to play out. "Are you three going to visit for a while before you go. . ." He struggled to say the next words. "Before you go to see Lionel?"

"Oh no. After meeting at Monica's, we're going over to see Lionel right away. Make a right here."

He sighed, wincing as he turned.

She touched his shoulder. "I'm sorry, Keith. But this is something that I have to do."

"I know." He swallowed hard. "And if this

is what you need to do, then so be it."

Minutes later, they pulled into the driveway of a charming house up the street from the waterfront. A multitude of flowers bloomed in front of the massive porch and sounds of a baby crying wafted through the open windows. Female voices followed by a deep male chuckle drifted into the yard, where white lawn furniture was arranged around the porch.

Karen rapped against the screen door a few times then opened the door. "Hey, guys, I'm here."

A tall pretty woman stood, patting the back of the infant in her arms. The baby whimpered before she stopped crying completely. "Karen. I was so worried about you. I'm glad you made it here."

Karen and the woman shared a one-armed hug. "You shouldn't have been worried."

A large woman with long, cornrowed plaits stood. "Well, somebody needs to worry. I think your going to see Lionel is a cuckoo idea." Her loud voice bounced off the walls. The heavy-set woman glared at Karen.

Keith decided he liked this woman. *Maybe I can convince her to talk some sense into*

Karen.

The other male in the room stood, speaking to the three women. "Y'all need to leave Karen alone. She's only doing what she feels she needs to do."

Karen smiled at her male supporter. "Thanks, John."

The tall man approached Keith, offering his hand. "I'm John French."

Keith shook his hand. "I'm Keith Baxter."

Karen gasped, looking at Keith with her pretty eyes. "I'm sorry. I've got so much on my mind that I forgot to introduce you. Keith, this is Monica and her husband, John, and this is Anna. And this little one is John and Monica's baby girl, Mica."

Keith shook hands with each adult, trying to ignore Anna's and Monica's curious stares. It might be best to explain why he came along. "Karen was tired this morning, so I told her I would drive her over here."

"Hmm," murmured Anna. "She was probably tired because she was tossing and turning all night, thinking about this trip." The large woman shook her head, her plaits swinging with the movement. "I'm telling you, Karen, this whole visit is a big mistake. You need to put that no-good man out of your mind."

Keith couldn't help the next words that slipped from his mouth. "Amen to that." He turned toward Karen. "Why don't you listen to Anna?"

Karen gritted her teeth. She gave him a sideways look, obviously exasperated. "Keith, I already explained everything to you this morning." She turned to Anna, looking her up and down as the large woman placed her hands on her ample hips. When Karen shrieked then hugged Anna, Keith wondered if she'd lost her mind.

"Anna, what a pretty engagement ring!"

Anna proudly modeled her left hand, showing the huge square-cut diamond ring on her finger. "Yes, Dean Love and I are getting married."

"When did you get engaged?" Karen sat on the couch.

"A few weeks ago."

Karen frowned. "Why didn't you tell me?"

"I wasn't sure if this was news you wanted to hear since. . .well, since Lionel was missing and all. Didn't want to make you feel bad since your engagement. . .ended on a bad note."

"But this is *good* news. This is something

I wanted to know." After admiring the ring for a while, Karen took the baby from Monica. "Hi, Mica," Karen greeted the infant with a smile. "Oh, Monica, she's so precious."

Monica grinned. "Can you believe she's already three and a half months old?"

Karen cooed and played with the infant until the child gurgled with laughter.

Keith relished watching Karen with the baby. "Do you like babies, Karen?"

Karen smiled and nodded before giving the baby back to Monica. Then, focusing on her best friends, she gestured toward the door. "Come on, let's go."

"Okay. I'll drive." Monica handed Mica off to her husband. "John, there's three bottles of milk for Mica in the refrigerator. If that's not enough, then there's a can of formula on the counter. Do you want me to make a few bottles of formula in case you run out?"

John smiled at his wife. "No, I think I can handle mixing formula if I need to."

"When you warm up her bottle, don't forget to test it on your wrist before you feed her." She looked at Karen. "I'm not sure how long we'll be gone."

"We shouldn't even be going," muttered

Anna, lifting her large purse from the floor.

Karen glared at Anna. "I need some answers. And you're my moral support. Can't you understand that?"

The three women continued talking as they exited the house. Seconds later, Monica popped back into the living room. "John, the box of diapers in the nursery is almost empty. I already bought some more, and they're still in the bag over there in the corner." She gestured toward the back of the living room.

"Monica, go. Mica and I will be fine."

She gave him a warm smile and kissed his cheek, then ran outside to join the other women.

19

Moments later, Keith sighed, watching the car disappear around the corner. "I almost feel like I made this trip for nothing."

"You really didn't want her to go, did you?"

"Obviously not. That loser doesn't deserve any visits from Karen after all he's put her through." He shook his head, watching as

John placed Mica in an infant seat on the floor. She gurgled, clutching a yellow rattle. "I should've stayed home. When Karen saw her friends, it's like I no longer existed."

John shrugged. "I know how you feel. When the three of them get together, it's almost like they're in a world of their own. That's just the way they are. They've been friends for such a long time, they're more like sisters than friends."

Keith huffed, still feeling dejected. "That doesn't make me feel any better."

John changed the subject. "Hungry?"

Keith nodded. "Yeah, I am. I had something at McDonald's early this morning before I did a repair, but I haven't had anything to eat since. I would've stopped on the drive down here, but Karen slept in the car the whole way." He frowned. "Said she didn't sleep much last night."

John shrugged. "I'm not surprised. Did you want to go and get something?"

"Yeah." He looked at Mica. "Won't Monica object to your taking Mica out of the house? She seemed to be a little worried about leaving her alone with you."

John's laughter filled the room as he took a large bag from the corner. He opened the sack of diapers and placed several into the black tote. "No, she won't care. I've taken Mica out lots of times. Monica's just a worried new mother." He took two bottles from the refrigerator and placed them in the bag. "I don't think she'll be hungry for a few hours. Monica just fed her, but I have to take a couple of bottles just in case."

Minutes later, John had Mica strapped into the car seat and Keith was sitting in the front seat with John. They pulled out of the driveway and John started talking about his family. "My life has really changed since I got married, but in a good way." Keith remained silent as John continued to speak. "Mica still gets up in the middle of the night to be fed at least two times. But according to the pediatrician, we can start giving her rice cereal within the next couple of weeks."

Keith grunted. "I'd start giving her the cereal now. Maybe it'll fill her up so she's not waking you guys up hungry in the middle of the night."

John chuckled. "That's what I told Monica, and she had a fit! She said that as new parents, we need to do follow doctor's orders."

Keith shrugged. "I guess you need to do

what you feel is best."

John turned a corner. "You like seafood?"

"I love eating—and making—just about any kind of food. I do a lot of cooking in my spare time. As a matter of fact, I bought some candy for all of you. I made it myself. Chocolate lemon buttercreams. The candy is in a cooler in my car. We can have some after we get back to your house."

"Sounds good. I love candy." They pulled into the parking lot of a seafood restaurant. John took a little time to unhook Mica's car seat, which doubled as a baby carrier. He then hoisted the diaper bag onto his shoulder, picked up the carrier, and locked the van before they walked into the restaurant.

John requested that they eat al fresco, so they were shown to a table outdoors. A large umbrella protected them from the bright sun and they had an exquisite view of the ocean. Beachcombers frolicked on the shore and tons of people played in the water. Keith made himself comfortable in the chair and enjoyed the wonderful view. He closed his eyes and sniffed.

John chuckled. "What are you doing, man?"

Keith grinned. "Thinking about Karen." Without mentioning is divinity school search, he briefly told John about the time he'd spent with Karen at Virginia Beach. "Karen asked if I'd ever noticed how the beach smelled. It smells good out here, briny."

After they were seated, he placed Mica's carrier between them. The brown-skinned baby looked at Keith, her mocha-colored eyes full of curiosity. Her full lips reminded him of a rosebud, and when she opened her mouth and smiled, drool spilled down her chin, prompting John to wipe it with a cloth.

The baby continued to smile at Keith, gripping a rattle. Keith, returning her grin, stroked her cheek. Her skin was soft like feathers. "She's a cute little thing."

"Thanks." John opened his menu. "I think she resembles Monica, but Monica said she looks like me." He shrugged. "I guess we'll find out who she takes after when she grows up."

"You don't have any other kids?"

John hesitated. "Before I got saved, I lived with a woman and she got pregnant. We had a son...and...well..." he took a deep breath. "My son died a few years ago. He had a brain tumor and he was only twelve."

"I'm sorry, man. That must've been rough." It'd been tough losing his dad, but, he couldn't imagine fathering a child, and the child be sick, and not live through adulthood. He wondered how his own faith would be tested if something like that were to happen to him. Could he still embrace God after suffering such a traumatic loss? The entire situation proved hard to even imagine, but, he figured he needed to do all that he could to imagine how others were suffering, figuring out how to spiritually advise them, especially when he fulfilled his calling to become a pastor.

"It was. In his later years, he'd become blind because of the brain tumor. It was one of the reasons why I shunned God." He then gestured to Mica. "But, to answer your question, Mica is me and Monica's first child."

Their waitress arrived, and Keith opened his menu. "I haven't even read the menu yet."

John closed his. "I can tell you what's good. Order the clam chowder and soft-shell crabs with potatoes and vegetables."

Keith gave his menu back to the waitress.

"I'll have everything he just suggested."

"Make that two," John said to their server. Nodding, their waitress left, returning moments later with their drinks and a basket of bread and butter.

Keith's stomach rumbled with hunger. "Do you mind if I pray before we eat?"

"Not at all. Go ahead."

Keith bowed his head. "Lord, thank You for this beautiful day at the beach. Thank you for this day of life and for the food we're about to eat. Also, Lord, I'd like to ask you to please watch over Mica, John, and Monica. Be with these new parents as they raise their first child." He paused, gathering his thoughts. After a deep breath, he prayed, "And, Lord, please let your Holy Spirit be with my friend Karen. I'm sure you know this is a difficult day for her. May she truly feel Your strength and guidance today. Amen."

"Amen." John looked at Keith as if trying to figure him out. "Thanks for praying for Monica and me. Parenthood is really taking a toll on us. It's not a bad toll, just different."

"I can imagine. I hear that all the time."

John buttered a piece of bread. "So, a lot of your friends have kids?"

Keith shook his head, squeezing lemon

juice into his water. He took a sip before responding. "I have one close friend who's expecting his first. But I hear a lot of new parents from my church talk about how their lives have changed."

"Do you and Karen worship at the same church? Is that how you two know each other?"

Keith's heart skipped a beat, realizing that Karen had probably not even mentioned him to her friends. *Maybe she has no feelings for me at all. Maybe she's still in love with Lionel.* Shaking off his thoughts, Keith finally responded to John's question. "I'm Karen's mother's next-door neighbor. When I moved in, Karen's mom, Doris, and I became friends and started attending the same church. She doesn't drive, so sometimes I'd take her grocery shopping and back and forth to services. Then Karen moved in with her mom, and she and I became. . .acquainted. For a while now, she's been helping me out with the youth ministry. I love working with teenagers, and I'd like to lead a church one day, Lord willing."

Soon their food arrived. As they ate, Keith again told John about the day he'd spent with Karen, except he also mentioned his divinity school visit. "We had a great time together, but. . . well, I'm afraid she's still in love with Lionel. Maybe after this visit, she'll be able to get him out of her system."

As they were finishing up, John finally spoke. "Wow, it sounds like you have a lot on your plate. Do you know where you want to go to school?"

"I'm still not sure. I'm researching colleges, trying to decide which is best for me. If I have to relocate, then I'll do it. I'm hoping by the time I decide, I'll know if there's any chance between Karen and me. I wouldn't be able to ask her to come with me if she still has feelings for Lionel." He glanced at the exquisite view of the beach as the waves tossed onto the sand.

John sighed. "I was once in a similar situation, in more ways than one."

"Really? How so?"

They were interrupted by the waitress bringing the bill. John pulled out his wallet.

Keith shook his head. "I've got it."

"No, that's okay. I've got it."

After they agreed to split the bill, paid it, they found an empty bench on the boardwalk. Not ready to head back to the house, they sat to enjoy the view of the beach. John took Mica out of her car seat and fished one of the bottles out of the bag. Keith recalled that Monica stated the bottle needed to be heated, but, surprisingly, the baby guzzled the bottle, seemingly not caring that her drink was unheated. John watched his daughter suckle her bottle for a few minutes. "I used to be an agnostic."

Keith frowned. "Really?"

"Yes."

"How did you hook up with Monica?"

"Well, remember I told you my son was blind before he died?" Keith nodded. "My son learned Braille and so did I. I became a tutor for blind kids shortly after my son's death. Monica has a blind nephew. She had to take care of him for a while. When he started having trouble in school, Monica brought him to me. As I explained, I tutor blind children in my spare time. As soon as we met, Monica and I were attracted to each other, but we couldn't date because of my agnostic beliefs."

"Sounds rough."

"It was. Keith, the most important day of my life was when I finally accepted Jesus as my Lord and Savior." He continued telling about how Monica had told him to go to a class at her church. The class was for new believers and for those seeking Christ. As Mica finished her bottle and then he placed her over his shoulder and gently patted her back so that she could burp, he finished telling Keith about how he'd come to accept Christ.

"That's an awesome testimony, John."

"Thanks." John gently rocked Mica to sleep before strapping her back into her car seat. "After I got saved, I wanted to join a traveling ministry to speak to other agnostics around the world." He shrugged while staring at two seagulls fighting over a piece of bread. "I wanted to make up for lost time, but I finally saw that was a skewed way of thinking and that God was calling me to stay right here and minister to the kids on the college campus. . .and marry Monica." He paused. "So, I can understand your feeling called to serve God in ministry. And I also know what you're going through as far as Lionel is concerned."

Keith frowned. "What do you mean?"

"Well, two years before I met Monica, she was involved with a guy named Kevin. I think she was still in love with him when they called it quits. Kevin got engaged months after their breakup, and when I met Monica, he still worshipped at her church. He'd bring his wife and infant to the services."

Keith shook his head. John's situation certainly did mirror his own, and he had to wonder if the Lord had led him to John today. "So, what did you do?"

"I confronted her about it. I think part of the problem was she never really had a conversation with Kevin about what had happened between them. He just broke up with her, and there wasn't really any closure." He glanced at a family strolling on the boardwalk. "As I think about it, Karen's in the same situation. She was in love with Lionel, she switched churches—"

"She switched churches?" Karen had not told him that. He'd just assumed she'd met Lionel through her church home.

John nodded. "Yeah, Karen used to worship at Monica and Anna's church. The three of them had gone there for years. That's how they met, doing the soup kitchen together. But when Lionel came along, he insisted Karen worship with him at his large megachurch, especially since they'd gotten engaged and all, and Karen agreed." John paused for a few seconds. "Anyway, since he disappeared, there was no way for Karen to have closure with Lionel. At least in Monica's situation, Kevin was still here, although she was never engaged to him—unlike Karen, who thought she was going to be spending the rest of her life with Lionel. Then Karen found out Lionel was being accused of embezzlement and, on top of that, a womanizer. Man, desertion, embezzlement, and two-timing. Talk about a triple blow." John shook his head. "That's a lot for somebody to go through, to find out those things about your future mate, somebody you proclaim to love—and who proclaimed to love you. No wonder she wants to see Lionel. How else is she going to put it all behind her?"

Keith thought about John's words. "I guess I can kind of understand why she'd do it, but it's kind of scary in a way, too."

"Scary how?"

"Well, I almost feel like she'll see that dude and then she'll find that she still has feelings for him. That in spite of the fact that he stole money and cheated on her, she'll still want to get back with him and work things out, especially since they're engaged and all. Then he'll just end up hurting her again.

That's something I couldn't bear to witness."

"Man, you don't know that'll happen. We'll just have to wait and see what God has in store. If you want my opinion, I honestly don't think Karen will take Lionel back. She's intelligent and has high self-esteem. I think she'll see Lionel's true colors and put the whole situation into perspective. That'll help her bring closure to their relationship. Then, once Lionel is out of her system, she'll be ready to move on."

Keith closed his eyes for a few seconds, silently praying that there was truth to John's words.

20

As Monica pulled into the parking lot of the police station, Karen wrung her hands. Her heart pounded as hard as a galloping pony. Goodness, could this day be any more stressful? "I feel so angry and nervous right now."

Anna folded her arms in front of her. "Humph. Maybe the Lord is telling you that you don't need to be seeing that no-good man."

Monica glared at Anna. "Anna, Karen has already made up her mind. What she needs now is our support." The three women unbuckled their seat belts, but before they got out of the car, Monica made a suggestion. "Don't you think we need to ask God for some help this afternoon?"

Karen sighed, giving Monica a small smile. "Thanks, Monica. I'm so nervous that I didn't even think about praying."

The three women joined hands and bowed their heads. Monica then prayed, "Lord, please be with Karen as she visits Lionel this afternoon. Please let Your Holy Spirit guide her and protect her during this difficult time. Amen."

"Amen," both Karen and Anna responded.

The three women exited the vehicle and entered the police station. When they approached, the female worker sitting behind the desk pushed her glasses up on her nose, giving them a bored look. "Can I help you?"

Karen nodded. "We're here to see Lionel Adams."

The woman glanced at the threesome. "The inmate can only have one visitor at a time."

Monica pulled Karen into a hug. "We'll be waiting out here for you, praying while you're back there, okay?"

Karen nodded, gazing at her two best friends. "Thanks." After checking Karen's ID and searching her purse, the attendant led Karen into a room with three tables. Each table had two chairs. Karen clutched her hands together, silently praying, her heart beating faster. The female attendant left, and seconds later, the door squeaked open. Karen turned to see a police officer leading Lionel into the room.

She gasped, hardly recognizing Lionel with his hair, now longer and being worn in dreadlocks, full mustache, and beard. His scruffy, haggard appearance was a stark contrast to the neat, immaculate, clean-shaven man she used to date.

Surprise tinged his dark brown eyes. "Karen. I didn't think you'd come to visit me."

She just couldn't say a word. She eyed Lionel as he sat in the chair.

The officer grunted. "You've got twenty minutes."

Karen nodded toward the retreating officer then turned toward Lionel. "I can't believe it." She finally managed to say something. She couldn't stop staring at Lionel. So, *this* was the man whom she was going to marry?

"Can't believe what?"

She sighed. "You look terrible." She shook her head, not wanting to waste any of her precious twenty minutes asking questions about his drastically altered appearance. "Lionel, I've come for some answers. First off, why did you steal the money? And why did you date me while you had feelings for Michelle?"

Lionel frowned, rubbing his eyes. "The church owes me."

"What?" What he'd said made no sense.

"I said the church owes me. God owes me."

Well, it appeared that Lionel had lost his mind when he'd gone missing. He was talking crazy right now. Perhaps she should tell the police that they needed to contact a psychiatrist. Lionel was delusional and he obviously needed help. "What are you talking about?"

He folded his arms in front of him, his expression angry. "You know I mentioned to you that while I was growing up, my mom got involved with a weird church?"

Karen nodded. "What's that got to do with your embezzling church funds?"

He sighed. "What I didn't tell you was that my mother gave those church people everything! Everything! They said all members needed to support each other." He stared at the wall, his voice becoming rough. "Soon there was nothing left to give. My mom got sick, and they didn't do anything to help her. Instead of finding a doctor, they said we could just pray over her and make her better. They said the money belonged to the church, and we didn't need to be wasting it on a doctor."

Karen swallowed, shocked. "Then what happened?" she asked softly.

Tears slid from Lionel's dark brown eyes as he continued to speak. "She got worse and then she died. God died that day for me, too."

Karen sniffled, her eyes welling with tears. She took Lionel's hand. "Lionel, that doesn't sound like a church. That sounds like a cult."

He waved her comment away. "Church, cult, religion. It's all the same."

Karen shook her head, sending up a silent prayer for Lionel's soul. "No, it's not all the same. You can't blame God because your mom got mixed up with the wrong religion." She squeezed his hand. "Why didn't you tell me all this before?"

"Nobody knows now except you and Michelle."

She dropped his hand, feeling as if she were going to faint. Trying to quell the anger and sorrow welling up within her, she closed her eyes and said a silent prayer, asking for God's guidance. When she felt a bit calmer, she opened her eyes. "Lionel, when did you start dating Michelle? Were you—*are* you—having an affair with her?"

He wiped his wet eyes, and seconds later, he'd regained his composure. "Yes, I am. Remember when I went to a finance seminar downtown about a year ago?"

Karen frowned, recalling the event. "Yes, what about it?"

"That's where I first met Michelle. I was attracted to her and we started talking. That's when we exchanged phone numbers and I started seeing her. Remember when I told you I was working late on the weekends and in the evenings?"

"Yes." Karen's heart skipped a beat.

"Well, I wasn't always working. I'd be with

Michelle sometimes." He continued to glance at Karen, propping his chin in his hand. "As I got to know her better, I finally told her about my religious background and how I was angry about my mother's death. After we'd had sex one night, she told me that her family had been mixed up with a strange religion, too."

Karen's mind was spinning. She checked her watch, aware of the seconds ticking away. "Why did you start going to church in the first place if—if you're not a Christian?"

"I joined because I planned on stealing from the church eventually." He lowered his voice. "I've stolen from a church before, but it wasn't for this amount of money. They never prosecuted me because they never found out about what I'd done."

"How could they not know?"

He sighed. "There are ways to hide those kinds of crimes. When I told Michelle about what I needed to do, and that the assistant treasurer position was open, I had her apply. And they hired her. She wanted to help me steal the funds, but when she saw the amount of money they had in the church, she didn't want to pilfer the small amounts that I was taking." He folded his arms in front of his chest. "She convinced me to steal a much larger amount. I told her it was harder to cover your tracks when you steal thousands of dollars like that, but she told me we could pull it off."

Karen's mouth dropped open. "And you believed her?"

"Yes. We figured we'd steal the funds and then resign from our jobs a few months later."

"Then what? Find another church to steal from?"

He shrugged. "Probably."

"Are you even sorry for what you've done?"

He sighed. "Like I said, the church owes me. Do you realize how much money my mother gave to the one we used to belong to? They said prayers and said that God could cure my mama, but she's dead now. These churches owe me for my pain and suffering!"

"Oh, Lionel. Don't be angry at God. You need to give Him a chance—"

"Don't talk to me about God! I don't want to hear it," he said slowly.

"What about Michelle? Did she turn herself in, too? Where have the two of you been all this time?" She rushed to ask her questions because time was running short.

"I'm almost ashamed to tell you, but since I've put you through so much, I believe you have a right to know."

"Know what?"

"When I discovered the church had found out about our crime, Michelle contacted her brother in Washington State. He's an ex-con. He told us we could stay with him until we figured out what we were going to do. Since I've been over in Washington for the last few months, I've had time to think. I found out about the warrant for my arrest, and..." His face hardened as he turned to gaze at the wall; then he looked back at her. "Karen, even though Michelle and I had lots of money in Washington, we were arguing all the time. And then when I started thinking things would be worse for me if I got caught, I got scared. So, I turned myself in. So did Michelle." He shook his head. "I'm still scared about going to prison, but I did what I had to do."

The guard spoke from behind the closed door. "You got two more minutes."

The next words rushed from Karen's mouth. "Did you care about me?"

His brown eyes glistened. "Karen, I did have feelings for you."

"Then why, Lionel? Why did you turn to someone else?"

He looked down at the table. "I had an affair with Michelle because I knew you wouldn't have a sexual relationship with me because of your religious beliefs. But while I was hiding out with Michelle, I still thought about you."

The news rocked Karen's world, and she struggled to keep her feelings in check. "Do you love her?"

"Who, Michelle?"

She nodded.

He sighed. "Not really. The only reason I ran away with her was because, well, when the church found out about what we'd done, I was scared."

"Lionel, be honest with me when you answer this next question. Did you ever love me?"

"Yes," he whispered.

"Are you serious?"

"Yes, I loved you and I thought we'd have a decent life together."

She narrowed her eyes. "But you're not a believer. Plus, what about stealing from the church? How would we have had a marriage if you were a thief?"

"Karen, I didn't think I'd get caught. I didn't think you'd ever find out about my deceit."

She removed the engagement ring from her purse. "I think it's only fair that I sell your engagement ring and give the money back to the church." She squeezed her palm hard, enclosing the ring within her hand. Tears rushed to her eyes, and she blinked the moisture away.

The officer stepped into the room. "Time's up!" Karen stood and walked out of the room.

Karen rushed into the lobby, wiping her eyes. Monica and Anna rose as one, pulling her into their arms. Anna gave Karen a few tissues as they made their way to Monica's vehicle.

"Are you okay?" asked Monica.

Karen shook her head. "No, I'm not okay. Monica, I know you want to get back to Mica, but could we stop for coffee for a few minutes? I really need to talk to you guys alone right now."

"No problem," Monica responded.

Soon they were sitting in Starbucks, drinking steaming cups of coffee. Karen cradled her mug, trying to stop her hands from shaking.

Anna finally broke the silence. "What did Lionel say?"

Karen took a deep breath then told them what Lionel had said about his mother's religion and her death.

Monica gasped. "That sounds like a cult to me."

Karen nodded. "That's what I told him. He just sounded so angry and bitter. Because of all that's happened, this is going to be hard for me to do, but I'm going to continue to pray that Lionel finds Jesus."

"Amen to that," mumbled Monica. "What else did he say?"

Karen then told them about his meeting Michelle and getting her on board as the assistant treasurer.

Anna sipped her coffee before speaking. "So, Michelle joined the church, too, just to steal money?"

Karen shrugged. "Apparently. I only had twenty minutes to talk to Lionel, so the information he gave me was kind of sketchy."

After Karen finished relating the rest of her conversation with Lionel, Anna asked, "Do you think he was really telling you the truth about loving you?"

"I don't know. I guess. Everything he said is like this huge knot in my head. I need to think about it, sort everything out. I guess I should praise God for allowing me to find these things out about Lionel before we were ever married. It's a blessing that the church discovered his crime."

Monica touched her hand. "Now that you've visited him, do you think you can put this whole thing behind you?"

"I already put it behind me for the most part." She spoke of how she'd come forward at her mother's church, asking God to help her with the pain and bitterness she harbored against Lionel. "Since Lionel turned himself in, I felt the Lord leading me to come and see him and get some answers."

Anna placed her cup on the table. "And now you have all your answers. Do you think you'll be going back to visit Lionel?"

Karen shook her head. "No. I just wanted to speak with him one last time." She glanced at her watch. "I know Keith wanted to get back to Annapolis today. He rearranged all of his clients so that he could bring me down here today."

Anna gasped. "Oh my goodness. We've been so busy discussing your meeting with Lionel that you haven't even told us about that cute man who drove you down here. What's his name again? Keith?"

Karen nodded. "Yes, Keith Baxter. He's a good friend of mine."

Monica asked, "Is he the man your mom was telling me you were involved with?"

"We're *not* involved."

As Anna threw her head back, laughing, her body bumped the table, causing Karen's coffee cup to topple. The hot coffee splashed onto the table and Karen's clothes.

Karen jumped up. "Ouch!"

Anna hurried for napkins to mop up the spill. "I'm sorry, Karen." Karen waved her comment away. "That's okay."

"Let me buy you another cup," Anna offered.

She shook her head. "I didn't even really want that one." After they had resettled into their seats, Karen told them about Keith. "He's just a good friend who's been there for me. We work together in the youth ministry at his church."

Anna said, "Well, you're more than just friends if he's rearranged his work schedule and driven you down here."

She shook her head. "No, we're just. . .friends." She frowned.

"What are you thinking about?" asked Monica.

"This morning, Keith tried to talk me out of visiting Lionel. Then he wanted to know if we could be more than just friends."

Anna folded her arms in front of her chest. "If you ask me, I think he's already a better man for you than Lionel. I can tell that he likes you. Is he honest and trustworthy, and, even more importantly, is he a Christian?"

Karen shifted in her chair, uncomfortable in her damp, coffee-stained pants. "Yes. He wants to be a preacher and is searching for a divinity school. He and his twin brother have had a falling out, but he's working to heal the rift. You know, it's funny. Initially, I didn't think he was interested in me. But now, after our conversation this morning, I know that he'd like for us to date."

"Are you going to?" asked Monica.

Karen shrugged. "I'll have to think and pray about it. I do like him." Karen was silent as she played with her empty coffee cup, still trying to digest all that she'd discovered about Lionel that day.

21

When they returned to Monica's house, Monica immediately scooped up her baby while Anna pulled Karen into a hug. "I have to go. You know you can call me if you need anything."

Karen returned her friend's hug. "Thanks for coming with me today, Anna. It really meant a lot to me."

Monica was occupied with Mica as Keith

rushed toward Karen, his eyes full of questions, questions she didn't feel like answering. She touched his arm. "I'll be right back."

She went upstairs and used the restroom. Afterward, she entered John and Monica's guest bedroom, wanting to spend some time alone. Fatigue swept through her as she sat in the wooden chair by the desk. After her visit with Lionel, she hadn't wanted to face Keith.

She glanced down at her stained pants. She wanted to change into a fresh pair of pants since the huge coffee stain was still a little damp. Perhaps she could borrow Keith's car and drive to Wal-Mart to purchase a new pair of pants before they drove home. She again thought about the conversation she'd had with Lionel, and a tear escaped from her eyes. While she was wiping the moisture away, a strong knock sounded on the door. It was probably Monica coming to check up on her. "Come in."

Her heart skipped a beat when Keith strolled through the door. The scent of his aftershave filled the small room with musky sweetness, and his warm caramel-colored eyes were full of concern. "Are you okay?"

Remaining silent, she stood and walked to the window, where she lifted the bright yellow curtain and stared down at the street. Keith walked to the window and stood beside her. She focused on the beach in the distance. Maybe if she stared at the beach really hard and remembered the good times she'd recently shared with Keith, she'd settle down and her nerves wouldn't be so rattled. She blinked several times, refusing to look at him, hoping to hold any further tears at bay.

"You're crying." He touched her hand. "Your hands are shaking. What did that…What did Lionel say to you?" The question slipped from his mouth like a quiet whisper, soft, yet demanding at the same time.

Heaven help her. She needed to be honest with him. She needed to let him know how she was feeling. She finally dropped the curtain and plopped down onto the queen-sized bed. "He said lots of things."

He sat on the bed beside her, taking her hand. "Like what?"

Taking a deep breath, she told him about her conversation with Lionel, eliminating his proclamation of love.

"Karen, that's terrible."

She nodded. "I know. I feel so bad for Lionel. I never realized he'd been through so much. I knew his mom had died when he was a child, but he never told me what really happened until today. At least now I know the reason why he stole from the church. He blames God and all religions for what happened to his mother. It's wrong for him to think that way, but I'm glad he finally told me."

"Do you still have feelings for Lionel?"

She squeezed his hand. "I feel bad for him, and I'll pray for him to accept Jesus, but I—I don't love him romantically." She took a few moments to gather her thoughts. "I started to let my bitterness go the day I came forward at church during Easter services. I did the best that I could without having Lionel around to talk to and find out what happened. I feel even better now that I've spoken to him."

Keith paused for a few minutes. "Do you think he still has feelings for you, even though he ran away with another woman?"

She sighed. "He said that he loved me but felt forced to flee with Michelle because of the church finding out about his theft."

"Do you believe him?"

She shrugged. "I suppose. It's hard to say."

"Well, thanks for telling me about your meeting with Lionel. That means a lot to me." He looked away, his shoulders drooping.

"Keith, what's wrong?"

Continuing to hold her hand, he turned back toward her. "I know you have a lot on your mind with all that Lionel has told you, but I wondered if you would consider what I asked you this morning."

"You mean about us seeing each other more, outside of the youth ministry?"

He nodded. "I really like you, Karen. Since I've accepted Christ and made a lot of changes in my lifestyle, you're the first woman I've liked enough to pursue a relationship with."

When she remained silent, he continued. "We can take it slow. We can see each other as friends. Is that okay with you? Karen, don't you like spending time with me?"

"Yes, Keith, I do, and I'd like to get to know you better, but are you sure you don't have any feelings for Melanie?"

"I already told you she's like a sister to me and that's it. I wouldn't lie to you about something like that. Nor about anything else for that matter."

She touched his shoulder, feeling bad about offending him. "I'm sorry, Keith. I'm afraid my experience with Lionel has made me skeptical as far as men are concerned."

"Well, I'm not Lionel. I already told you that I'd never disrespect you like that."

Suddenly Karen realized how good a friend Keith had been to her since she'd relocated to Annapolis, and how well he'd treated her. "Keith, I'm sorry." Her voice wavered as she struggled to keep her emotions in control.

"Sorry? Why?"

"Because you've done so much for me. You've shuffled your clients just to drive me to Ocean City." She didn't mention the fact that he'd done that just so she could see another man. "I've been ignoring you since you've been here, and I never even said thank you for doing this for me." She again touched his shoulder. "So, thank you. I appreciate all you've done."

"You're welcome. But don't you understand, Karen? I'd do anything for you." She nodded as a tear ran down her cheek.

Keith brushed her tear away with his finger. "Are you sure you're okay?"

She sighed and nodded again. Keith got up and pulled a few tissues from the box on the desk. He gave her the tissues and she wiped her eyes. Then he pulled her into his arms. He glanced down at her pants. "What happened to your clothes?"

She told him about their visit to the coffee shop. Karen pulled at her damp pants. "My coffee spilled on my clothes. I wondered if I could borrow your car and go to Wal-Mart to get some new pants before we head home."

"Want me to go to Wal-Mart for you?"

"No, I'd rather get them."

"I'll drive you over there if you want." He continued to caress her with his amazing eyes. "Have you eaten today?"

She thought about the toast she'd had for breakfast. "Not since early this morning."

"Aren't you hungry?"

She shook her head. "No, not really."

"Well, you need to eat something." He pulled his keys from his pocket. "We'll say good-bye to your friends, and then I'll take you over to Wal-Mart. Afterward we'll stop and get you something to eat."

She grabbed her purse and followed him out the door.

At Wal-Mart, Keith watched Karen rifle through racks of clothing. He could tell she wasn't really paying attention to the items. Her body was in Wal-Mart, but her mind was obviously elsewhere.

"Couldn't you have borrowed some pants from Monica? And returned them when you saw her again?"

She gestured toward her petite, cute frame. "Well, Keith, we're not exactly the same size. Plus, I'm not sure when I'm coming back to Ocean City."

He supposed that was a stupid question on his part. Monica's clothes would probably fall right off Karen.

"Would you like me to help you look?"

She quickly shook her head. "No, that's okay. I'll be done in a minute." She finally settled on a pair of blue jeans. "After I buy these, I'll change, and then we can get something to eat."

"Okay."

She glanced around the store.

He touched her shoulder. "Are you sure you're okay? Did you need anything else?"

"No, that's it."

After she had paid for the jeans and changed in the restroom at Wal-Mart, they got back in his car. "Where did you want to go and eat?"

"There's a fast food place not too far from here. Why don't we eat there?"

He started the ignition. "I have no idea where I'm going, so you'll need to tell me how to get to the restaurant."

"Sure."

As Karen gave him directions, Keith noticed the town was full of tourists trekking along the busy sidewalks. Curious about Karen's past, he asked, "So how did you happen to be living here in Ocean City if you were raised in Annapolis?"

"I went to the University of Maryland at Eastern Shore for college."

"You have a bachelor's?"

Her pretty eyes widened at his reaction. "Yes, I'm sure you're surprised about my degree since I'm a hairdresser, just like I was surprised to find out you have an MBA and you're a plumber."

He chuckled. "That's true. So how did you happen to become a hairdresser?"

He continued to drive, savoring the sweet

sound of her voice as she recalled her college years. "Girls that lived in my dorm used to come to my room and get their hair done. I was doing it so regularly that I had to start charging people for it."

Keith interrupted her. "So, you were doing hair without a license?"

"Yes. But since I wasn't working in a salon, it wasn't an issue at the time. I taught myself how to do hair, and I guess it was a natural talent I had." She continued, "When I graduated, I realized I liked doing hair more than studying to receive my degree in business administration. I wanted to work in a salon as a beautician, but I couldn't do that without a license."

He shrugged. "So, what did you do?"

"I went to cosmetology school. While I was there, I apprenticed in a salon under another hairdresser in Ocean City."

"So, you moved to Ocean City after you graduated from college?"

"Yes. Since the University of Maryland isn't too far from here, I decided to move to this area after graduation. Then I started worshipping in the same church as Anna and Monica. We worked in the church's soup kitchen regularly, and that's how we became friends."

He pulled into the parking lot of the fast-food place and cut the ignition, still lulled by the sound of her voice. "When did you accept Christ?"

"When I was in college. My mom and dad were always regular churchgoers, but I never truly placed Him first in my life until I was living in the dorm."

"Did something happen to make you accept Him, or did you just finally bite the bullet and decide you wanted to follow Jesus?"

"Well, the whole story is kind of long."

"I'd like to hear it if you don't mind."

"Okay, well, when I was away from home, in college, I realized I'd only gone to school because it was expected of me, and although I then found I had a great outlet by doing hair and finally getting paid for it, I still felt like my life was missing something." Passion began to fill her voice. "Then my roommate started socializing and studying with a campus Christian group. They had a Bible study in my dorm room sometimes. My roommate invited me to come, and I found that through the Bible study, my questions about God and salvation were answered. I started poring over the scriptures because, even though I'd been to church all my life, I'd only read a few verses here and there. I'd never read the entire Bible, nor actually spoken with others who knew so much about the scriptures. So, one night during Bible study, I told the group that I'd accepted Christ." Her voice wavered, and tears now filled her eyes. "I'd found the piece that was missing from my life. A passionate relationship with Him." She wiped her eyes. "You know, I'm glad you asked me that question, Keith."

He smiled, taking her hand. "Why?"

"Because you've just reminded me about the most important day of my life."

He smiled then gestured at the restaurant. "Come on, let's go get something to eat."

Hand in hand, they walked toward the restaurant.

22

After seeing Lionel, Karen continued to pray for his salvation and that he would find help for the bitterness he still harbored against those who were responsible for his mother's death. As the trial came near, both Monica and Anna kept her abreast of what was transpiring in Ocean City. She eventually learned that Lionel had been sentenced to two years in prison. She felt a little sad but held out the hope that Lionel would seek religious counsel while in prison and one day accept Christ.

During the late summer, Karen and Keith helped with the annual youth picnic held on the church grounds. Karen watched Keith as he poured charcoal onto the grill. As the teens munched on pretzels and chips while waiting for the meat to get done, Karen thought about Keith's divinity school search. She knew he was narrowing down his choices and would, within a few months, make his final decision.

"Hey, Karen." Amanda approached, sipping a soda. Karen smiled at the young girl.

"Hi, Amanda."

Amanda grinned. "I saw you staring at Mr. Keith."

Karen looked away, wishing the teen hadn't caught her gawking at Keith. Wanting to steer the conversation in another direction, Karen changed the subject. "How have you been lately, Amanda?"

Amanda shook her head, still smiling. "No, you can't go changing the subject by asking about me. What's up with you and Mr. Keith?" She gestured toward the teens eating their snacks. "We've all been wondering if you two are dating or what?"

Karen thought about the frank and honest discussion she'd had with Keith after their impromptu day trip to Ocean City. "Yes, we're dating, but we're taking it slow."

The girl raised her eyebrows. "Taking it slow?"

Karen had noticed that since Amanda had broken up with Ron, she'd stopped wearing so much makeup and had ceased wearing provocative clothing. "Yes, we're getting to know each other as friends."

The girl pursed her lips. "I wish me and Ron had done that. Maybe if we'd taken things slow, we'd still be together. He called me last night, wanting to reconcile, but I told him no, even though it was hard."

Karen sighed. "I know we've talked about this before—"

"I know, I know, I need to stay celibate until I get married. I've learned my lesson. Believe me."

Karen mentally sighed, saying a quick prayer for Amanda's well-being.

Keith approached, pulling Karen into his

arms, kissing her cheek. "I got one of the guys to man the grill for a few minutes. What are you two ladies talking about?"

Amanda giggled then said, "Girl talk," before rejoining the other teens.

Keith chuckled. "I hope I didn't interrupt anything."

Karen sighed, basking in the scent of Keith's aftershave as she settled into his strong arms. "We were just talking about. . .stuff."

"What kind of stuff?"

Karen swatted his shoulder. "Girl talk, like she said."

One of the teens turned on the radio, and praise and worship music soon floated on the warm summer breeze.

Later, Karen watched Keith as he served up burgers and hot dogs. Afterward, they played a competitive game of softball. The teens munched on a huge batch of Keith's chocolate lemon buttercreams for dessert. Once the picnic was over and all of the food had been put away, Keith and Karen drove home in his car.

After he pulled into his driveway, he turned to Karen. "I was going to watch the game tonight. Want to join me?"

"Sure."

Suzie greeted them as they entered his house. After letting the large dog out into the backyard, he threw a bag of popcorn into the microwave and grabbed two sodas from the refrigerator. He plunked ice cubes into the Styrofoam cups before pouring their beverages. Moments later the scent of buttered popcorn filled the room.

After they were settled into the living room and he'd turned on the game, Karen ate a few kernels of corn before taking a sip of soda. Headlights shone into the living room, announcing an unexpected visitor.

"Who in the world can that be?" Keith mumbled, standing. Before he opened the curtain, he smiled a little bit. "Maybe it's my brother."

Karen's heart skipped a beat, hoping that it was, indeed, Keith's brother coming to make amends with his twin.

"Oh man." Disappointment filled his voice as he dropped the curtain.

"What's wrong?"

"It's Melanie."

"Oh." Karen wondered about Melanie often. After Karen had told Keith about Melanie's behavior following her haircut, he'd called her to check up on her. It turned out Melanie's fiancé was too controlling and was constantly telling her what she needed to do to change herself. After her fiancé had forced her to lose her locks and then quit the youth ministry, Karen wondered what else he would make her give up.

She rapped on the front door and Keith opened it. "Hi, Melanie, I'm kind of—"

She stormed into the house, not giving him a chance to finish. After wiping her tear-streaked eyes, she noticed the popcorn, sodas—and Karen. "Oh!" Her brown eyes widened. "I didn't realize you had company."

Keith's expression softened as he looked at Melanie. Jealousy, as thick as pea soup, flowed through Karen.

Melanie turned to Keith. "I—I could come back later if you want."

Karen sighed, gathering her purse. "That's okay. I need to get going anyway."

Keith shook his head. "No, Karen, don't leave." He looked at Melanie. "You can tell me anything you want in front of Karen. There are no secrets between us."

Melanie sat down, wiping away her tears. Karen brought her a box of tissues.

"I'm sorry to interrupt," Melanie said

through her tears.

Sitting beside her, Karen said, "It's okay. Melanie, Amanda was just asking me about you today. She said a lot of the teens have missed you since you quit the youth ministry."

Keith sat across from the women in a chair, staring at Melanie. "What's the matter? Why are you crying?" His deep voice was full of concern.

Melanie glanced at both of them before responding. "I just gave Duane his engagement ring back."

Karen gasped. "You broke your engagement?"

The woman nodded. "Yes."

"Why?" asked Karen.

Melanie sighed. "It just got to the point where he'd criticize everything I said or did. I—I couldn't do a thing without wondering if Duane would get upset or angry. After you live like that for a while, it makes you tired."

Keith shifted in his chair. "What did Duane say?"

Melanie frowned. "You don't want to know. Let's just say he wasn't pleased."

"So, you're not going to see him anymore, at all?" Karen just couldn't resist asking that question. In spite of what Keith had said she still wondered if Melanie still secretly held out hope that Keith would date her someday.

Melanie shook her head. "Karen, I can't. He made me cut all my hair off. He hated my talking to my friends. He just wanted me to focus on him and do whatever he told me to do."

Keith stood and squeezed Melanie's shoulder. "I'm glad you broke things off with him. We're here for you if you need anybody to talk to."

For the rest of the evening, Melanie unburdened her heart to Keith and Karen.

The following Tuesday, Karen entered the salon and was greeted by her coworkers. After placing her equipment out on her station, she removed her bucket of curlers and made sure she had enough supplies for touch-ups and hair colorings for the day.

When it was almost time to break for lunch, Deidre spoke in an amused tone. "Karen, you have a visitor."

Karen turned, pleasantly surprised to find Keith standing at the receptionist's desk. He walked back to her station, holding a dozen brilliant scarlet roses surrounded by baby's breath. "Keith. I didn't realize you were coming." He certainly was a refreshing sight to see. Some of the other stylists were openly gawking at him. She wanted to take his hand and scream at the top of her lungs...*he's mine.*

He shrugged. "I came to see you."

"But you never come to visit me at work."

He glanced around the shop for a few seconds, as if he was nervous. He gave her the bouquet. "Here, these are for you."

"Thanks." She sniffed the flowers before laying them on her counter.

"Mmm, mmm, mmm," mumbled Sheronda. "Your man must've done something wrong if he brought you those flowers for no reason."

Karen gritted her teeth, having grown tired of Sheronda's unfounded innuendos. Ignoring the remark, she focused on Keith.

"Actually, I, uh, came by to get a haircut."

Karen chuckled. "You want me to cut your hair?"

"Yeah, if you don't mind. My barber's out of town and I need a cut." He touched his head, and Karen gestured him over to the chair.

"Sit down."

Keith sat and Karen placed a cape around him. She looked until she found her clippers in the bin. She then plugged them in and turned them on. As the light buzz filled the space, she admired Keith's profile as he waited for her to cut his hair. Warmth enveloped her when he glanced toward her, catching her staring at him. She swallowed, saying the first thing that came to her mind. "Sit still."

He chuckled, giving her a warm smile. "You don't have to tell me to sit still. When I was five, I moved around in the chair so much that the barber accidentally nicked my ear with his clippers."

While smooth jazz floated from the speakers, she smiled at him, touching his hair before running the clippers over his perfectly shaped head. They continued to buzz as she cut his hair low. She glanced at his face periodically, and when she gazed at his full lips, she wondered how it would feel to French kiss Keith Baxter.

She pushed the thought from her mind, finishing her task. "All done."

Keith glanced in the mirror. "It looks

perfect." His caramel-brown eyes shone with warmth as he turned his gaze to her. "It's the best haircut I've ever had."

After they had settled the bill and he'd paid the receptionist, he came back to Karen's station. "Do you want to go out to lunch?"

Karen checked her watch. "I only have a half hour."

Keith shrugged. "That's enough time. We can get hot dogs from the vendor outside and sit on the bench to eat."

After they'd gotten their food, Keith blessed their simple meal and told her what was on his mind. "I'm sorry about the other night."

"Do you mean when Melanie came over?"

He nodded. "I know we were going to watch the game together, but I didn't want to make her leave when she was so upset."

"That's okay. I understand."

"I'm glad that you stayed."

"I just hope things work out for her now that Duane is out of the picture."

"Yeah, she called me last night and told me that she's moving."

"Moving?"

"Yes. She quit her job and she's moving to

North Carolina to open a health food store with her cousin. She'd talked about doing this before she met Duane, but after they got engaged, it was just one more dream he'd squelched."

"A health food store. . . That's a big switch."

"I think it'll be good for her. This is something she's passionate about, and I think it'll help her to heal. She wants to keep in touch with both of us." They ate in silence for a few minutes before Keith spoke again. "You know, I wanted to ask you something."

"What's that?"

"Both of us get up pretty early in the morning . . ."

Karen shrugged. "Yeah, so?"

He finished his hot dog before taking her hand, squeezing her fingers. "You know how much I love cooking, especially after my early morning workouts."

Hmm. It'd be interesting to find out where this whole conversation was leading. "I know." She fondly recalled the first time she was in Keith's kitchen and the way he'd fixed breakfast for her. She also recalled the first time she'd tasted his delicious candy.

"Well, I hate cooking just for one. So, I was

wondering if you wanted to come by for breakfast."

She smiled. "Sure, when? Tomorrow?"

He squeezed her hand. "Not just tomorrow, but. . .every day."

Karen widened her eyes, wondering if she'd misheard him. "You want me to come to your house every day for breakfast?"

"Why not?"

"It would just seem weird, my coming to your house every day to eat breakfast."

"Really?" He was silent for a few minutes as he continued to hold her hand. "I think it'd be kind of nice. But if you don't want to see me so often, that's okay."

He frowned, and Karen wondered if she'd hurt his feelings, so she rushed to explain herself. "I didn't mean it would be weird in a bad sort of way, just weird as in different."

He tilted his head. "What do you mean?"

She balled up the paper from her hot dog, tossing it into the bin beside their bench. "Keith, in my thirty years of life, I've never seen anybody I was dating every day."

"What about Lionel? Didn't you see him every day?"

Karen shook her head. "No, not even Lionel. I guess the thought of my seeing somebody every day is just so new, I–I'm not used to it." She squeezed his hand, giving him a huge smile. "But I think I like the idea."

His frown eased into a smile. "Really?"

"Yes. Although we're already seeing each other once or twice a week, I have wanted to spend more time with you, but I just wasn't sure how often you wanted to see me."

"So, is that a yes? You'll start coming by for breakfast every morning?"

Her smile widened. "That's a yes." Her heart pounded as Keith leaned closer, and then he kissed her on the mouth.

23

Over the following couple of weeks, Keith eagerly awaited Karen's coming to his home and sharing breakfast with him. He soon found that the more time he spent with Karen and the better he got to know her, the deeper he was falling in love with her.

As September rolled around, he took Ms. Doris out to the nursery to get her fall chrysanthemums on sale. It had been the first time he'd needed to take Ms. Doris anyplace in months. Since it was Saturday, Karen was busy at the hair salon, and Ms. Doris had been anxious to get her flowers planted.

"Keith, don't these look lovely?" she said, fingering the nursery's white and orange blossoms. "I'm going to set these out in my backyard as soon as we get home. My plants have really been thriving since Karen's been watering them every day."

Keith just smiled, his mind elsewhere.

As they drove back to his house, Ms. Doris tapped his shoulder. "Too bad Karen had to work today. It would've been nice having her along."

"Yes." His mind elsewhere, he barely paid attention to Ms. Doris.

Doris chuckled. "I've noticed that Karen has been eating breakfast at your house lately."

Keith smiled, nodding while he drove. "Yes." He was falling in love with Karen, but he wasn't sure if he should tell Ms. Doris his true feelings.

"Karen seems much happier now. She's changed since she's renewed her faith and started spending more time with you."

"Yeah. And you know, although I didn't like the idea at first, I think it helped her to visit Lionel. She obviously needed closure. And now that he's out of her life for good, I think she's on the road to healing." *And hopefully falling in love with me.*

Doris chuckled again.

Taking his eyes off the road for a second, Keith caught her smile, which made him smile in return. "What are we grinning about?"

Doris hesitated a moment then said, "Keith. . .we're not just neighbors, but friends, right?"

"Right." *Where is this leading?*

"And friends can discuss anything with each other, right?"

Suddenly feeling uncomfortable, Keith replied with a hesitant "Right..."

"So, I'm going to come right out and ask you. Are—are you in love with my daughter?"

While Keith's mind began to scramble for an answer, he felt the heat rise in his cheeks.

Doris smiled knowingly. "You *are*, aren't you?"

Keith grimaced. "Is it that obvious?"

"To me it is. I take it you haven't told

Karen yet."

Keith took a deep breath. "Here's the thing. I don't know if I should yet."

"Why not?"

"Well, for one thing, I've only known her for six months."

"Well, that's true, but—"

"And for another, she's on the rebound. I mean, she just came out of a really bad relationship with a man who deceived her in so many ways. He cheated on her, committed a crime, and then disappeared."

"Yes, Keith, but—"

"Well, I really find it hard to believe that she would be ready to hear words of love spoken by another man."

Doris was silent, her smile now faded, her brow furrowed. Finally, she looked directly into his eyes. "Well, all you say is certainly true. So, there's really only one piece of advice I can give you."

"What's that?"

"Pray about it."

"I have. But I haven't gotten a clear answer to that, nor to…"

"Nor to what?"

"Kyle. My brother."

"Oh, right. Kyle. Have you seen him since

that day you stopped in at his town house?"

"No. I call him occasionally, and he sometimes answers the phone, which I guess is a good sign. But our conversations are so stilted. It's like we're strangers instead of brothers."

"Hmm. Any new ideas of why your father arranged the inheritance the way he did?"

"Well, I did stop in to see Dad's lawyer, hoping he'd remember something—anything—any reason as to why Dad changed his will. But I came up empty-handed." He sighed heavily. "I tell you, Doris, my plate is full. Between my feelings for Karen, the issues with Kyle, the search for a school, and taking care of my own business, I feel like I've got so much more than I can handle." He pulled into his driveway.

"What you need, Keith, is to spend an entire day alone with the Lord."

"You think? An entire day?"

"Sometimes that's what it takes. Trust me. I know what I'm talking about."

24

The following Wednesday, Keith took Doris's advice. He got into his car and drove to Sandy Point State Park. Bible in hand, he grabbed a beach chair from the back of his car and set it up beneath the trees, staring at the Chesapeake Bay beach in the distance. Since it was near the end of the season, the place was almost deserted. Sitting in the cool breeze, listening to the leaves rustle in the early autumn wind, he read his well-worn Bible, gaining comfort from the scriptures. He chose to fast that day. Although his stomach rumbled with hunger, he knew he needed to focus on God, and ignore food, at least for the time being.

After a full day of thoughtful reflection, he finally bowed his head and folded his hands. *Lord, I've got quite a load on my shoulders. I want to discuss it with You, one item at a time.* He sighed then continued praying silently. *Okay, Lord. First, You know I want to tell Karen I love her. But I don't know if she's ready to hear it right now. Give me wisdom in this situation, Lord. Let me know when the timing is right.* He paused, pressing his hands tighter together. *And, Lord, I miss my brother, Kyle. I don't know how to heal the rift between us. On top of that, he hasn't accepted You, Lord. Touch his heart. Give me the right words to say. Help me to convince him of the gift of eternal life. I ask all these things in Jesus' name. Amen.*

Feeling as if a huge weight had been lifted, Keith raised his head, his eyes taking in the billowy clouds above him. As he reveled in the cool breeze, the sound of the water slapping the shore, and the wonder of God's creation, his phone buzzed, pulling him out of his reverie. Removing the phone from his pocket, he glanced at the display, noting the unfamiliar number. "Hello?"

"I'm looking for Keith Baxter?" He frowned upon hearing the professional female voice.

"Speaking. How can I help you?"

"You're listed as a contact for Lawrence Baxter."

Keith's heart skipped a beat when he heard his father's name. "Contact for what?"

The female sighed. "For his safe-deposit box here at the bank. He needs to make a payment if he wants to keep it open. We've called his phone number, but it's been disconnected. And the payment notice we sent to his house came back as undeliverable."

"Which bank is this?"

"The Annapolis Bank."

"Ma'am, my father died almost a year ago. Is it possible for me to have access to his safe-deposit box?"

"Sir, that's fine since you're listed as a point of contact. It'll also help us if you'd bring a copy of your father's death certificate as well as your driver's license." She then told him the address of the bank.

Keith packed up his chair and Bible, jumped in his car, and drove away, trying not to break the speed limit, anxious to find out what was in his father's safe-deposit box. After stopping at his house to get his father's death certificate, he drove to the bank. When he arrived, he was ushered into the back of the building, where an employee opened the box for him then pointed to an empty room.

"You're welcome to go in there and look at the contents of the box."

Keith stepped into the room and opened the small box. Inside were a few pieces of jewelry as well as a cream-colored envelope. He opened the envelope and found a notarized letter addressed to him, dated a few weeks before his father's death. Keith read:

Dear Keith,

I know that my remaining days upon this earth are few. With that in mind, I feel called to write this letter, to tell you some things I seem unable to say.

First, thank you for showing me the way to the Lord. That is something for which I will be eternally grateful. How I wish I could change the past, but I feel content in knowing my future lies in heaven with God.

Second, I know that Kyle has been troubled since his breakup with Andrea. And my being diagnosed with cancer seems to have sunk him into an even deeper depression. I also know he hasn't been handling his finances very well lately. Keith, I'm worried about your brother's physical and spiritual well-being. Please be there for him. Help him sort things out. And try to show him he needs to lean on Jesus.

And lastly, because of your brother's erratic behavior, I don't feel comfortable leaving him a lot of money right now. So, I'm leaving the bulk of my estate to you, hoping and trusting that you will allocate your brother's half whenever you feel he is responsible enough to handle it.

Keith, you are an extremely levelheaded young man, and I'm proud of you. I trust that you will seek the Lord's guidance in this matter.

I love both you and Kyle with all my heart. May God bless you both, in this world and the next.

In Christ, Your father, Lawrence Baxter

Keith held the letter, wondering why his father chose to leave it in the safe-deposit box and not tell him about it. *Perhaps this is what Dad was going to tell me about just before he died.* Keith stood in the room, lost in thought. A knock sounded on the door. "Sir, we're about to close the bank."

Keith stepped out of the room, holding the contents of the box. "May I take these things with me?"

The woman nodded. "Yes, when your father filled out the paperwork for the box, he listed you as the party who should have possession of the contents in case of his death. Can you step to my desk for a few minutes? I'll need you to sign some forms."

After Keith had signed the appropriate papers, the banker placed the safe-deposit contents into a large padded envelope. Keith carried the envelope to his car and drove home.

25

When Keith arrived at his house, he brought his vehicle to a screeching halt. "Lord, You've certainly been busy today answering my prayers," he muttered, recognizing the classy black Lexus sitting in the driveway.

Taking a deep breath, he exited his car and walked toward the front door of the house. Kyle sat on the porch, beer bottle in hand. Placing the bottle on the wooden planks, he then stood, staring at Keith.

Keith swallowed, unsure of how to greet his twin. He eyed the beer bottle again, recalling that the last time he'd seen Kyle, he'd been hung over from a drinking binge. He lifted the bottle, noting it was empty. He set it back down then examined his brother's eyes. "You're sober."

Kyle lifted his dark eyebrows. "I only had one beer. Give me a break." The brothers stood on the porch observing one another until Kyle spoke again. "Come on, I wanted to talk to you about something." Kyle gestured toward the house.

Keith thought it weird, Kyle inviting him into his own home. But his brother had always been like that, taking the lead, trying to tell Keith what to do.

"Go on in." Keith gestured toward the front door.

Kyle grunted. "You're not thinking, little brother—the door is locked. I tried it when I got here."

Rattled, Keith pulled the keys out of the pocket of his faded blue jeans. Keith walked the few steps to the door, opened it, and strolled inside, his brother following close behind. Suzie ran up, tail wagging as she barked a greeting to the brothers.

Bending down to pet the dog, Kyle's gaze swept the room as if appraising the value of its contents. "Have you been spending the money that Dad should've left for me in his will?"

Keith gritted his teeth, trying not to lose his temper. This was not the best way to start this visit. Placing the padded envelope on the coffee table, he decided to change the subject. "I haven't eaten all day. Did you want to order a pizza or something?"

"You don't cook anymore?"

Keith shrugged. "I still cook, but I don't feel like making anything right now. Do you want to get a pizza or not?" He couldn't help the impatient tone of his voice. Why couldn't his brother simply answer the question instead of being difficult?

Kyle looked away for a few seconds before responding. "Yeah, that's okay with me."

Keith ordered the pizza then grabbed a couple of Styrofoam cups. After putting ice and soda into the containers, he brought them into the living room.

Kyle looked at the soda then stood. "I've got to get something out of my car." He soon returned with the rest of his six-pack of beer.

"Man, take that beer out of this house." His voice exploded in the house like a loaded bullet. Kyle wasn't one to take him seriously unless he raised his voice. He just wanted to avoid his brother getting sloshed, acting ugly, as he'd acted when he'd run into him at the restaurant.

"I'm not going to get drunk and act stupid. I promise."

"I don't want alcohol in this house. Take it out, now." Standing face to face, the brothers glared at one another until Kyle eventually left the house and returned empty-handed.

For a few moments, they sat in tense silence, Kyle continuing his survey of the living room. Spotting the brochures for divinity schools on the coffee table, Kyle picked one up and began flipping through it. "You plan on going back to school or something?"

Kyle had always been good about doing that. After they'd had an argument or disagreement, he smoothly changed the subject, almost as if he was trying to make Keith forget about what had just transpired.

Between sips of soda, Keith told Kyle about his search for the right divinity school, ending with, "It's something I feel called to do."

Kyle scoffed, tossing the brochure back onto the coffee table. "What's that mean anyway?"

Before Keith could respond, a knock sounded on the door. "That must be the pizza." He strolled to the door and moments later returned to the living room, pie in hand. "Let's go into the kitchen to eat." After Kyle was seated, Keith removed two paper plates and napkins from the cupboard. He sat down, silently blessing their meal, then opened the box.

For a few moments, the brothers ate. Then Kyle broke their silence by repeating the question he'd asked earlier. "What do you mean by you feel *called* to go to divinity school?"

Keith chewed and swallowed, carefully choosing his words. "I feel this is what God wants me to do."

Kyle removed another slice of pizza from the greasy box. He smirked. "How do you know God wants you to do it? Did He knock on your door, come in, and say, 'Keith, I want you to go to divinity school'?"

Striving to overcome a growing feeling of

exasperation, Keith spoke calmly. "I just feel in my heart that this is the direction the Lord wants me to go, the path He wants me to take."

Kyle grunted, finishing another slice of pizza.

Questions continued to riddle Keith's brain like popping kernels of corn, and he again wondered why his brother had chosen to show up on this day. Before asking what Kyle wanted, he decided to tell him about what happened earlier. "I got a phone call from the bank."

Kyle frowned. "What bank? What are you talking about?"

He stood, gesturing toward the living room. "Come on, I'll show you."

He opened the envelope and dumped the contents on the coffee table. "Dad left me this letter. It was in a safe-deposit box. I didn't even know the box existed until today. The letter...I—I want you to read it."

Kyle read in silence, his mouth set in a tense line. When he finished, he lowered the letter, his hands dropping to his sides.

For a few minutes, no words were spoken. Then Kyle looked at him. "I didn't realize Dad knew about my finances."

Knowing their father wouldn't lie, but wanting Kyle to admit he had a problem, Keith looked directly into his brother's eyes. "So it's true?"

Kyle nodded. "The part about my finances is, but not the part about my being..." He picked up the letter again and read, " 'Troubled.' "

"Kyle, we both know your drinking has gotten worse." When Kyle remained silent, Keith asked the question that had been burning in his mind ever since he'd seen Kyle's car in his driveway. "Why are you here?"

Kyle hesitated, suddenly looking unsure. "I—I came to ask you a favor."

"Well? What is it?"

"I'm in little bit of a bind."

Keith narrowed his eyes. "What do you mean by *little*?"

"Well, maybe it's not so little."

"Well, what's the matter?"

"My home is in danger of being foreclosed."

Keith widened his eyes. Shaking his head, he sank into the nearest chair, feeling like a fool. *And I actually thought you'd come over to patch things up between us.* He sighed then looked up at his brother. "So, I guess you want money."

"Well, yeah. I'm glad to find out you weren't dishonest about getting Dad to change his will." He pointed to the letter. "He said you could disperse the funds as you see fit. I think you should give me my half of the money now. No matter what Dad thought, I'm not a child."

"Listen, Kyle. For a minute, let's forget about the money. Let's talk about us, about your not trusting me, about your having barely spoken to me since Dad died. You never even gave me a chance to tell you my side of the story."

Kyle rolled his eyes. "Okay, little brother, what's your side?"

"Remember the day that Dad died?"

Kyle frowned. "Is this your way of giving me a guilt trip?"

"A guilt trip?" What was he talking about?

"Yeah. Are you deliberately trying to make me feel guilty because I was in the Virgin Islands while you stayed here, taking care of Dad?"

Keith sighed. "No. I'm just trying to get you to understand where I'm coming from."

"Whatever." Kyle took a seat across from

Keith. "So, go ahead. I'm listening."

Keith struggled to gather his thoughts, recalling their father's last month of life. "The day Dad died, he wasn't feeling well. Remember how he didn't want to go into a nursing home?"

"I remember," Kyle whispered, his face softening. "He said he wanted to die at home."

"Right. Well, he'd been feeling worse than usual that day. The hospice nurse came, checked him out, gave him some medicine. He told me he wanted to talk to me about something important, but he'd been in so much pain the day before that he was very tired. He managed to tell me he felt bad about the way he'd raised us, and he wished that we could have been tighter, as a family."

"Dad never cared about being closer to us."

"Yes, he did. He just never showed us. You know, I learned a lot about Dad that last year. Anyway, he always figured that having a lot of money would prove how much he cared for us." Keith paused, his eyes misting with tears.

"What else did he say?"

"H–he told me he'd made some changes to

improve things in the household."

"Huh?"

"I know. He started talking to me like I was a little boy instead of a grown man. Said things were going to change around here. At first I thought the medicine was affecting his mind, so I told him to take a nap and we'd talk about it later."

"And when you went back to check on him, he was gone," Kyle said softly.

"Yeah. I never got a chance to ask him what he'd meant. When the will was read, I was just as floored as you were. But I honestly think that he was going to tell me about this letter, or maybe give me the key to the safe-deposit box."

"So, you didn't have the key?"

Keith shook his head. "No. I didn't even know the box existed until today. But now we know why he did what he did." He gazed at his twin. "It looks like it was a smart move, too, especially with your present situation." He paused. "Listen, Kyle, I hate that this money issue has come between us. I miss talking to you. I—I miss your being in my life."

Suzie, having awakened from a nap, sauntered into the living room and placed her large head on Kyle's lap.

"See, even Suzie notices you're not around anymore." Keith tried to make light of a serious situation. But his brother didn't even crack a smile. Keith hesitated. "Kyle, now that we both know what happened, can't we just move past this and start...well, start being brothers again?"

Kyle remained silent, petting Suzie's fur. "We'll always be brothers. I just don't know about us being. . .friends."

For a moment, Keith was stunned, his heart cut to the quick. Then he said softly, "Kyle, the very fact that you thought I lied in order to cheat you out of your inheritance. . ." He shook his head then said, "Have I *ever* given you a reason to mistrust me before? I mean, have I ever lied to you?"

The room filled with silence, each brother lost in thought. Abandoning Kyle, Suzie approached her master, begging for food. Keith went into the kitchen and poured food and water into the dog's dishes before returning to the living room.

Kyle sighed. "Look, I know you've never lied to me, but you still need to give me my part of the inheritance." He glanced around the house again. "Have you been spending my share of the money?"

"Kyle, I told you all this in the letters and e-mails I sent you the first few months after Dad died. I haven't touched a dime of your money."

"Well, I need it. If I lose my house, I might end up having to move in here with you. Do you really think that's a good idea?"

Exhaustion, mingled with exasperation, racked Keith's body. *Lord, give me strength.* He ran his fingers through his hair. "What happened to your money anyway? Dad left you some in his will, plus you're running a law firm, and I know what salary you're bringing home. Why—and on what—are you spending so much money?"

Kyle shrugged. "It's something to do, I guess." Keith frowned. "I like spending money, traveling, buying things, taking women out. You know me, Keith."

"The Kyle I knew spent lavishly but always paid his bills. What happened to you?"

Kyle shrugged. "I—I guess it all started when Andrea left. I was so hurt. I couldn't stop thinking about her. So, I started drinking. Just a little at first. Then when I realized that wasn't enough, I started doing anything to take my mind off of her—trips, extravagant gifts for women, you name it. The bills started coming in fast and furious. I just let them pile up, I guess. Next thing I know, Dad gets sick and dies. Then guilt piled on top of the pain, and I just got further and further behind on the bills. . .and I started drinking more heavily." Kyle sat slumped in his chair.

"Well, big brother, let's take it one step at a time. First, how long do you have before you lose the house, and how much do you need to keep it?"

"Six weeks before they foreclose." He then told him the amount of money he needed.

The exorbitant sum made Keith's head spin. He whistled. "Well, I don't want you to lose your house, but I need to think and pray about it."

"You're asking God about giving me money that's rightfully mine?"

"Yes, like I've told you, I go to God for all of my major decisions."

The twins sat silently for a few minutes before Kyle spoke. "Well, I guess I have no choice but to wait for your answer." After an uncomfortable silence, Kyle cleared his throat. "So, are you still seeing the woman I saw you with at the restaurant?"

"Yes." Good thing his brother changed the subject. "I'm in love with her."

"Really? Does she feel the same way?"

Keith frowned. "I don't know. Haven't told her how I feel yet."

"Why not?"

"I think the Lord wants me to wait a bit."

"Well, be careful, little brother. Remember what happened between me and Andrea."

"I'll be careful. Karen's been through a lot over the last year, and I just want to be sure she's ready to hear what I have to say." He paused for a few seconds. "She's been coming over every morning for breakfast."

Kyle raised his thick eyebrows. "Really? She drives over here every day just to eat with you?" He playfully swatted Keith's shoulder.

Keith grinned, shaking his head. "She doesn't drive over; she walks."

"Huh?"

Keith pointed toward the kitchen window. "She lives right next door. I was friends with her mother before I ever met Karen. She moved in this past spring. She'd just gotten out of a really bad relationship. Turns out her *ex*-fiancé was not only an embezzler but a two-timer."

"Man, and I thought I had a bad breakup."

"Yeah, well, she's doing a lot better now than when she first came to Annapolis. She's been helping me with the youth at church. And then somewhere along the line, we started dating." He smiled again. "And every day we have early morning breakfasts, then evening walks with Suzie. If everything works out the way I'd like it to—I mean, if it turns out she feels the same way about me— then I'm hoping she'll be my wife and come with me when I start divinity school. But we'll just have to wait and see."

Kyle stood. "Well, I've got to get going. I hope things work out with you and Karen."

Keith nodded, pulling his brother into an impulsive hug. "Thanks. I love you, bro. I'll be in touch. And you...Don't be a stranger."

26

On her way over to Keith's house, Karen decided that tonight was the night. She was determined to find out what had been bothering Keith over the last few weeks. Just as she was about to knock on his front door, it opened.

"Hey there, gorgeous." Keith's initially brooding frown turned into a smile. "Suzie's ready for our evening stroll. Are you?"

"I sure am." She returned his smile.

Starting down the sidewalk together, a comfortable silence soon descended as each strolled along, lost in thought. As they turned a corner, Karen glanced at Keith's face in the streetlight. Suddenly it hit her. *Keith Baxter, I am falling for you. . .hard.*

As if reading her thoughts, he lurched to a halt, pulled her into his arms, and began kissing her. At first, Karen was stunned, as was Suzie, who began barking and nudging her nose in between them. Then all sense of time and place was lost as Karen melted in Keith's embrace. What seemed like hours later, he released her.

"Well..." She could barely manage to speak while she caught her breath. Kissing Keith Baxter...was oh so delicious. Ten times more delicious than his candy.

Keith, grinning from ear to ear, grabbed her hand and held on tight.

As they continued their stroll, Karen's wits began to return. But Keith was soon back to brooding. Karen tapped his shoulder. "Keith, are you okay? Is anything wrong?" No response. "Keith?"

He suddenly looked up from his study of the sidewalk. "Huh?"

"I asked you a question."

"Oh." He gave her a halfhearted smile. "Sorry. What was it?"

"I asked if anything was wrong?"

"Wrong? No, everything's fine." He lifted her hand to his lips, giving her a gentle kiss.

Hmm. Okay. Let's try some small talk. "I've got some news."

"Yes?"

"I got Amanda a job as a shampoo girl at the salon."

"That's nice," he said absentmindedly.

"Yes. She seems to like it."

"That's good."

"Yeah, she's a great girl. I'm so glad you got me involved in the youth program at church. I like spending time with them once a week."

"Mmm, yes. Me, too."

Finally, Karen gave up trying to have a conversation with Keith. *But when we get back to the house, I'm going to sit you down and find out what's going on.*

When they had circled back to Keith's house and approached the end of his driveway, he would have walked right past had Karen not stopped dead in her tracks.

"Did you want to make another loop

around the neighborhood?"

Keith, suddenly pulled from his reverie, lurched to a halt, then said, "Uh, no. Sorry." He cleared his throat. "Want to sit on the back porch for a while?"

"Sure."

Suzie played in the backyard while Keith and Karen sat in silence, the brightly colored leaves tumbling from the trees in the autumn breeze.

"Keith, if we're going to be having a relationship, you need to be open with me. What's been bothering you lately?"

They held hands. He began playing with her fingers. "Sorry, I know I've been a little moody lately. I've had a lot on my mind."

Karen shifted in her seat, suddenly uncomfortable. "Like what?"

"Oh, things, problems."

Karen cleared her throat. "Um, we're okay, aren't we? I mean, you don't have a problem with us, do you?" *Oh, please say you don't.*

Keith smiled and squeezed her hand. "No, honey. We're fine. It's just that I've been trying to figure out what to do about my brother's money. I know I need to let him have it, but I'm not sure how to go about giving it to him. Do I wait a month? A year?"

"Is that all?"

"Well, to me it's a pretty big deal. I mean, if I give him too much all at once, there's no telling what he'll do with it. What if he takes off to Cancun or goes on a drinking binge? And do I give him just enough to save the house now, see how he handles it, and then wait until next year to give him more?"

"Sorry. I know it's important, and I wish I could help you. But the only thing I think we can do is take it to the Lord and see where He leads."

Keith's eyes lit up. "You know, you're right. Do you remember the verse from Matthew, the one where Jesus says, 'If two of you on earth agree about anything you ask for, it will be done for you by my Father in heaven. For where two or three come together in my name, there am I with them'?"

"Yes. That's the one we've been focusing on at Devo."

"Right. Well, let's pray together right now and lift this problem up to God."

"Sounds great." *Lord, this man is a keeper.*

Keith took Karen's other hand, and beneath the light of a harvest moon, they lifted his concerns to God.

A week later, Karen headed over to Keith's house early in the morning, eager to see him. She walked right past her mother's autumn chrysanthemums, which needed no watering today since God had taken care of it the night before with a blessing of heavy rains.

Last night, Keith had told her he was making blueberry muffins, bacon, and eggs this morning, and she was looking forward to the meal—and seeing him. After she rapped on his door, Keith opened it, beckoning her inside. Suzie barked excitedly as Keith let the dog out to play in the yard.

"Hi, Karen." He kissed her cheek.

With a contented sigh, Karen stepped into the kitchen, the scent of blueberry muffins filling the air. She removed her light jacket. "Hi, Keith. You know, it's starting to get colder in the morning."

"I know. We're going to have to start wearing our heavy coats soon."

"Smells wonderful in here."

He chuckled. "Yes, this is Ms. Sonya's recipe. You know, I'd like to take you over to meet her and Mr. Terrance soon." He pulled the muffins out of the oven. "This is a lot of food. Maybe you can take some muffins over to your mom."

"Yes, I'm sure she'd like some."

He removed eggs from the refrigerator.

"You seem to be in a good mood," Karen commented.

He placed the eggs on the counter and returned to the table, temporarily abandoning his task. "Let's have a seat while the muffins are cooling off. I want to talk to you about something."

Curious, Karen sat at the table.

Keith took her hand, squeezing her fingers. "I think I've found a solution to my problem."

"Do you mean the problem with your brother's money?" He nodded. "What are you going to do?"

"Well, I called him last night. I'm going to give him his half of the money."

"Do you think he can handle that much cash all at once?"

"No, but I've worked that out, too. I'm going to give it to him over the next ten years in equal annual installments. But even before he sees one red cent, he's got to give me proof that he's getting financial counseling."

"Do you think that's the right thing to do?"

"Karen, I've done the best that I could. The rest is up to God. But you know, I feel like a huge burden has been lifted. This money issue has weighed heavily on my mind since my dad died. But since I've made my decision, I feel happier. And Kyle was definitely agreeable to the terms."

"I'm glad." She squeezed his hand. "Do you think he'd consider coming to church with you sometime?"

"I can't see that happening anytime soon. But we'll just have to wait and see. Meanwhile, we'll pray on it. At least my relationship with Kyle is a little bit better now."

Karen smiled, loving Keith's jovial mood.

He returned her smile. "I had something else I wanted to talk to you about, too."

"Really?"

"Yes." He pulled her onto his lap, kissing her cheek. "I love holding you, Karen."

She giggled, her heart beating wildly. "I like having you hold me, Keith."

He hugged her for a few seconds before releasing her. "Karen, I just want you to know that you're one special lady and that I'm in love with you."

Her heart skipped a beat. "What?"

He kissed her nose. "I love you, Karen Brown."

She smiled, euphoria filling her soul. "And I love you, too, Keith Baxter."

27

As the months passed and Christmas rolled around, Keith invited Karen over for a festive holiday dinner. Keith sliced the tender roasted chicken and served it onto real dishes – no paper plates for a special meal to celebrate Jesus's birth. He then proudly heaped mashed potatoes and gravy – both made from the recipes he'd learned from Ms. Sonya – onto their plates.

Fresh steamed vegetables and homemade rolls rounded out the meal. After he'd blessed the food, Karen eagerly sampled the meal.

"Oh, Keith, this is so amazing. I've never thought roasted chicken could taste so good."

He kissed her cheek before starting to eat. "I'm glad like it." Since Karen had relocated to Annapolis and had started eating with him regularly, she'd been happier. She'd also put on a few pounds. The extra weight looked good on her and it was nice to see her happy instead of the thin, brooding woman who initially showed up on Ms. Doris's doorstep. She also had said she enjoyed walking Suzy with him each night and was thinking about starting to jog regularly. He could imagine their exercising together, especially when the weather turned warm. "Hey, I wanted to ask you something. Remember you'd told me that you wanted to own your own salon? Well, are you still interested in doing that?"

She nodded as she reached for a roll. She slathered butter onto the bread. "Yes, but not now. The timing isn't right. I've been doing some more research and I've been talking to some other shop owners. I'd like to wait and learn more for at least another year before pursuing that dream."

"Are you sure?"

She nodded. "Yes. It's hard to get approved for a small business loan. There are some things that I want to do, business-related things, that will increase my chances of being granted a business loan. I just feel God wants me to wait a bit before pursuing my dream."

He nodded. "I can respect that." He reached over and took her hand. "Let me know when you're ready to pursue your dream. I'm here to help you in any way that I can."

"Thanks, Keith."

After they were finished their dinner, he offered sweet potato pie with fresh whipped cream for dessert. "Keith, this is so delicious." Karen loaded more cream onto her pie.

"Thanks."

After dessert they sat in his living room, gazing at his Christmas tree. "It's so pretty," Karen gushed. "Do you get a tree every year?"

"No, this is the first time I've purchased

one since I've been living alone." He pulled her into his arms. "I wanted to ask you something."

She smiled. "What's that?"

He reached into his pocket and pulled out a velvet box. When she opened the lid, her excited grin made his head spin. "Will you marry me?"

"Yes, I'll marry you!" She pulled him into her arms and kissed his lips. "I love you, Keith," she whispered.

"I love you, too, Karen."

She admired the ring now gracing her finger. "We need to go let my mother know!" Karen pulled her cell phone from her pocket. "She went out to dinner with some of the women from church, but I've got to call her and tell her the news." She put the phone on speaker after she dialed the number.

"Hi, Karen." Her mom's voice sounded in the living room.

"Mom, I'm engaged!"

"Oh, Karen." Her mother's voice wavered. "I'm so happy for you."

"Hi, Ms. Doris."

Her mother chuckled. "Keith, I already know you'll be a nice, respectable husband for my daughter. Congratulations, both of you."

After they rang off with her mother, Keith focused on Karen. "Our news wasn't a surprise for her."

"Of course, it was."

His eyes twinkled as he looked at her. "No, it wasn't. I asked your mother last week if it was okay if I asked you to marry me."

She playfully swatted his arm. "Oh, Keith, I'm not some young teenager. You didn't have to ask my mother's permission."

"I know, but I just wanted to be sure she approved."

"Well, you knew she would. My mother thinks highly of you, and I know she's grown fond of you since you moved in next door."

"Yes, that's true."

"Oh, Keith. I'm so excited." She grabbed his arm. "Do you think your brother will come to our wedding?"

"I hope so. You know, I asked Kyle to come by for dinner today, but he told me he couldn't make it. He said he had a date."

"Maybe he should have brought his date with him." She took Keith's hand. "I hope, eventually, that I'll be able to spend some time with your brother and get to know him. Is he still getting help for his drinking?"

Keith nodded. "He's been going to AA meetings and says he hasn't had a drink in weeks. And...well..."

"Well, what?" She continued to admire her ring.

Keith hesitated then said, "Kyle told me he'd come to church with us this Sunday."

Karen's mouth dropped open as she stared at Keith. "You're kidding."

Keith shrugged. "But don't get your hopes up. Kyle is known for breaking promises and changing his mind."

"That may be true, but to have him to agree to come to church with us at all is a big deal if you ask me."

"Yes, you're right." Keith dropped her hand and stood. "I'll be right back." He returned minutes later with a colorful brochure. "If you're agreeable, I'd like to enroll in Calvary Christian College for their fall term."

Karen smiled, glancing at the catalog, admiring the picturesque campus. "Where is Calvary Christian College?"

"It's in Waldorf, about an hour from here. We could move there if you'd like, but if you'd prefer staying here next door to your mom, I'll understand. I also wasn't sure how you'd feel about trying to find another job as a hairdresser in Waldorf. If you want, we can stay here, and I can always commute."

Karen hugged him. "Keith, if you feel the Lord is calling you to move to Waldorf, I'm okay with that. From my experience, it's usually pretty easy to find another job at a salon in a new area, but I'll admit that I have gotten used to seeing my mother every day."

"How about we compromise? We can move to Waldorf, but we'll drive down every Sunday to take your mom to church and spend the afternoon with her."

"That sounds good to me. Thanks, Keith." Happy tears slid down her cheeks as she hugged him.

Eight months later...
"Are you ready, little brother?"

Keith paced the dressing room at the church, feeling stiff and unnatural in his tux. He stopped walking and looked at Kyle, who was also in a tuxedo, ready for the wedding that was going to start in an hour. After a few moments, he answered his brother's question. "I'm about as ready as I'll ever be. I'm just grateful and blessed that the Lord brought Karen into my life. I am nervous, though."

Kyle pulled on his collar. "Yeah, I saw Karen and the rest of her bridal party arriving a while ago. Karen's a nice woman. I like her."

Keith nodded. "I'm glad you and Karen hit it off so well." He paused. "I know the wedding's going to start soon, but I just wanted to tell you that I'm glad we're getting along now and that you agreed to be the best man at my wedding."

Kyle looked away for a few seconds, continuing to tug nervously on his collar. "Yeah, since I've stopped drinking and started getting my life back on track, I guess it made it easier for us to settle our differences."

"Are you happy, Kyle?"

His brother sighed. "I feel better than I did eight months ago."

"But are you happy?"

"I know you're going to tell me that I'll only find true happiness by accepting Jesus."

Keith mentally sighed with relief. Although Kyle had not accepted Jesus, he had attended services with him and Karen a few times. And his voice was no longer full of disdain when they conversed about the gospel. Not wanting to push the issue, Keith simply clapped his brother on the shoulder. "Just keep my advice in mind."

"I will, Keith."

One hour later, the quartet played the "Wedding March" as Keith watched Kyle, Steve, and his church friend, Aaron, walk down the aisle. Anna, Monica, and Amanda then slowly followed, their matching royal blue gowns flowing behind them. Keith smiled with pride when Karen came forward. Her long lacy white dress contrasted nicely against her dark skin. Her large eyes were full of tears as she approached, holding a red floral bouquet in her small hands. She was so beautiful that Keith knew he could sit and look at Karen Brown forever. After Pastor Bolton performed the ceremony and they'd said their wedding vows, they shared a long, blissful kiss.

If you enjoyed Bittersweet Dreams, I'd appreciate it if you left a short, sweet review/rating on Amazon, Goodreads, and/or Bookbub! Reviews are often used

by readers to find wonderful books. Thank you!

Coffee and Kisses Excerpt

Chapter 1

2018

Rainy Jackson pushed her hair away from her dampened forehead. Such a hot, muggy day. She'd heard on the radio that morning that you could cook an egg on the sidewalk. She eyed the cruise ship in the distance. The cool water beckoned her. Maybe once she was on the cruise ship, and cooled down, she'd feel better. She sighed as she spotted a hot dog vendor. A mocha brown man strolled toward the vendor. From the back, it appeared he had the same swagger as her ex, Jordan. He even had the same suitcase and had the same haircut as Jordan.

Had Jordan found out about her cruise and had traveled from London, realizing he had made a big mistake, and now wanted to change her mind? No way could she board this ship if Jordan was going to be on board, too. He'd already told her that they were over. She swallowed as she rushed toward her ex, dragging her suitcase behind her. Her heart thudded like thunder as she yelled and grabbed the man's arm. "Jordan!"

The man grunted and turned toward her. The top of his soda snapped from the cup and the liquid spilled onto his clean shirt. The stranger's mouth dropped open as he glared at her. "You're not Jordan..." she whispered the words as shame, hot and fierce as the burning sun, filled her soul.

"No, I'm not. You're a nutcase woman, grabbing strangers like that. You should be ashamed of yourself." The stranger gave her one last glare before vacating the dock. She eyed him while he made his way toward the Miami street. Thank God he wasn't going to be boarding the cruise ship. She didn't think she'd have the courage to face him during this one-week cruise around the Caribbean.

She stood on the dock and winced as hot tears raced down her face. Maybe that man was right. She was a nutcase. She'd been so worked up, "seeing" Jordan again, she'd not even apologized to the stranger for grabbing him like that. What an embarrassment. Since her breakup with her ex-fiancé, she'd made this same mistake three times. Her best friends Sarah and Rachel had given her a ride to the dock. En route, Sarah had stopped at a light, and a tall, chocolate-brown man jogged past. He looked so much like her ex-fiancé Jordan she had to fight to stay in the car. She had pressed her hands together when he paused at the light. While running across the street, the jogger glanced at the car. She had frowned as she looked at the stranger, disappointed that her imagination was playing tricks on her again.

The first time it had happened was when she attended a gospel concert with Sarah and Rachel. She'd dropped her pizza and soda while grabbing the stranger's arm. He pulled away as Coke and food splattered on his white T-shirt. She muttered an apology as he disappeared in the crowd. Closing her eyes, she recalled the sweet memories of her ex-fiancé.

Clutching the handle of her suitcase, she sat on a bench and swiped her tears away. "Oh Lord, what have I done? Am I strong enough to go on this cruise alone? Lord, I need your strength, right now." She opened her eyes and looked toward the heavens. The vivid blue sky was dotted with huge fluffy white clouds. Her tears mingled with her sweat as she watched a flock of birds swoop through the sky. "Jesus. Help me."

Winston Michaels stood on the dock of the Miami cruise ship. He'd witnessed the beautiful brown-skinned woman, grabbing the stranger's arm. She'd obviously mistaken the stranger for somebody else. As he eyed her, sitting on the bench, crying, he'd not known what to do. She'd looked so shaken up. The stranger shouldn't have glared at her like that. The woman was obviously distressed and had made a mistake. Perhaps if the stranger had shown more kindness, the woman may not have resorted to tears.

He took a deep breath. He'd go over and try and offer comfort, maybe ask her if she needed a cold drink or something. As if she'd suddenly found energy, and courage, the woman stood up from the bench and walked toward the check-in counter of the cruise ship. So, this lovely woman would be boarding the ship. He'd try and talk to her later. She looked like she needed a friend, and it appeared she was traveling alone.

He popped the last two pieces of his favorite mocha-chocolate candy into his mouth. The delicious sweetness was soothing. He then sipped the last of his hot hazelnut coffee and threw the empty paper cup into a nearby trashcan. He sighed, thinking about his recent pain. If he saw this young woman on the cruise ship, he'd be sure to introduce himself. Looked like she needed a friend. Besides, if he talked to her, and focused on somebody else's pain, he might be more inclined to not focus on his own.

When Rainy Jackson embarks on a cruise to escape her two-timing ex-fiancé, she meets handsome, charming Winston Michaels.

Winston is trying to deal with his pain. A recovering alcoholic, he's not emotionally strong enough for a relationship. Can he assist Rainy with her ministry and learn to lean on God instead of alcohol?

Coffee and Kisses – *available now!*

Grab your copy today!

https://ceceliadowdy.com/coffee-and-kisseslp/

CECELIA DOWDY is an Amazon bestselling author who lives near Washington DC. She enjoys listening to old tunes with her husband and spending time with her son. Baking is one of her favorite passions. She loves experimenting with bread recipes using her sourdough starter. Serving homemade desserts to friends brings her joy. Her love of baking shines in her romance novels. When she's not in the kitchen, or spending time with her family, she's cooking up delicious faith-filled plots. Fans say reading her tasty novels makes them hungry. Sign up for her newsletter: https://ceceliadowdy.com/sign-up-for-my-email-list/

www.ceceliadowdy.com

Connect with Cecelia Dowdy

Join my mailing list! I will keep you updated about future releases:
https://ceceliadowdy.com/sign-up-for-my-email-list/

Let's discuss the Bible – visit my Sunday Brunch biblical discussions on my blog:
http://ceceliadowdy.com/blog/category/sunday-brunch

Please visit my website for more of my books:
www.ceceliadowdy.com/

You can also find me on social media:
https://www.facebook.com/CeceliaDowdyAuthor/
https://twitter.com/cdnovelist
https://www.bookbub.com/authors/cecelia-dowdy
https://www.tiktok.com/@cdnovelist

Other Titles By Cecelia Dowdy

THE BAKERY ROMANCE SERIES
http://ceceliadowdy.com/bakery-romance-series/
Loving Luke *(Book 0)*
Raspberry Kisses *(Book 1)*
Shades of Chocolate *(Book 2)*
Sweet Dreams *(Book 3)*
Sugar and Spice *(Book 4)*
Southern Comfort *(Book 5)*
Sweet Delights *(Book 6)*
Cinnamon Kisses *(Book 7)*

THE CANDY BEACH SERIES
https://ceceliadowdy.com/the-candy-beach-series2/
Caramel Kisses – *(Book 0)*
Chocolate Dreams – *(Book 1)*
Milk Chocolate Kisses – *(Book 2)*
Bittersweet Dreams – *(Book 3)*
Coffee and Kisses – *(Book 4)*
Rocky Road Dreams – *(Book 5)*

CECELIA DOWDY
HISTORICAL TITLES
http://ceceliadowdy.com/books/
The Baker's Bride
An Underground Railroad novella

The Doctor's Bride
A historical romance novella

www.ingramcontent.com/pod-product-compliance
Lightning Source LLC
Chambersburg PA
CBHW072045190726
48294CB00005B/1420